Luna faced the animal without fear. She marveled at its grace, even at rest. Its glossy coat shimmered in the fragmented moonlight. The paws, each of them as big as a man's two fists, were braced on the ground. The killing claws were sheathed and out of sight. It was a thing of deadly beauty. Black leopard.

The beast's mouth opened and closed once, and again. From the muscular throat came its soft growl. . . .

The eyes of the woman filled again with tears. They were not tears of sorrow and loss, but of joy. She took a step toward the big cat and opened her arms to it.

With a cry almost like that of a child, the leopard was upon her.

NASTASSIA KINSKI
MALCOLM McDOWELL
JOHN HEARD
ANNETTE O'TOOLE

A CHARLES FRIES Production
A PAUL SCHRADER Film

"CAT PEOPLE"

Screenplay by ALAN ORMSBY
Based on the story by DEWITT BODEEN
Special Visual Effects by ALBERT WHITLOCK
Music by GIORGIO MORODER
Director of Photography JOHN BAILEY
Executive Producer JERRY BRUCKHEIMER
Produced by CHARLES FRIES
Directed by PAUL SCHRADER

An RKO-Universal Picture
"CAT PEOPLE" theme sung by DAVID BOWIE
Lyrics by DAVID BOWIE
Music by GIORGIO MORODER

CAT PEOPLE

A novel by **Gary Brandner**

Based on the story by **DeWitt Bodeen**

FAWCETT GOLD MEDAL • *NEW YORK*

Prolog

The woman, Luna, stood outside her hut in the heat of the midday sun. She gazed with worried eyes down the slope to where the men of the village were holding council. The men squatted in a circle at the edge of a field of parched brown stubble, a field where once grain had flourished. Beyond the circle of men was a flat patch of hard, cracked mud, with only a shallow pool of brackish water at its center. This had been a broad, clear watering place shared by man and beast.

Behind her, the trees at the edge of the jungle, once green and lush, had withered into grotesque dead shapes during the terrible drought. Far across the plain, the snow on the peaks of the great mountains mocked the village's thirst.

Luna turned away from the men and stood for a moment watching her little boy at play. The child held a rock in his tiny brown fist. He made it hop along the dry ground, making happy little chirps with each hop. Feeling Luna's eyes upon him, the boy looked up and smiled. His teeth were white and even, his brown eyes clear. Luna returned the smile, but her own eyes were moist.

"Dog," the boy said in the language of the village. He held the rock out to Luna in the palm of his hand.

"I see," she said gently. "It is a fine dog."

The boy returned to his play. The woman said softly to herself, "Play your little games while you can, my son. Play and be happy today."

The council of the village men came to an end. Luna watched their faces as they rose and turned away from one another and walked silently to their separate dwelling places. Her heart turned cold when she saw the face of her man, Darak, as he came toward her. She turned away from him and, pushing aside the animal skin over the entrance, went into the hut.

When Darak entered he found her squatting before a clay bowl, stirring a thin mush for their evening meal.

"It is decided," he said.

"The giving of the children?"

"Yes."

"Is there no other way?"

"You know there is not."

"Can it not be delayed?"

Darak swept aside the animal skin at the entrance. The flat, hard heat blasted in at them.

"Delayed? You have eyes, woman. You have seen our animals die, our crops shrivel and fall away to dust. There is no water. The very jungle shrinks from our village like a poisoned thing."

"The rains will come again."

"The rains will never come while the dark gods are angry. Our village has offended them. We must pay the forfeit or we will all perish."

"But the children . . ."

"It is the law. It has always been the law."

Luna searched her man's face for any sign of hope, then she dropped her gaze.

"Our son?" she said, although she knew the answer.

Darak nodded. He pulled the animal skin back to shut out the sun. His face was unreadable in the shadows. "He is one of those chosen."

"Our only child," Luna said.

"I know."

"He is innocent of any offense to the dark gods."

"That does not matter. The decision is made. It cannot be changed."

As the sun began to sink behind the far mountains the children selected were gathered in the clearing at the center of the tiny village. There were two little girls and two boys. One of the boys was the son of Darak and Luna. The children looked around at the unsmiling faces of the people. They were puzzled, yet excited by this new adventure.

Luna, as the mother of one of the chosen children, was allowed to stand at the inner circle, and was not shunted to the back with the other women. Her little boy saw her and smiled.

"Game?" he said.

With an effort Luna kept her face empty. "Yes," she said, "it is a game."

"Mother come?"

"No. I cannot come this time."

"Father come?"

"Your father will be with you for a little while."

"Not mother?"

"No. It is not allowed."

For a moment the little boy's face clouded. Then he forgot about it and joined the other children in giggling and acting foolish, enjoying the attention they were getting.

The last red sliver of the sun winked out on the shoulder of the highest mountain. Darkness swept over the plain and the village and into the jungle.

"It is time," said the Leader of the village.

The women stepped back, and the men moved in around the four children. Darak looked back for an instant at Luna, then quickly turned away lest he betray some unmanly feelings.

One of the men began chanting an ancient lullaby. The children quickly took it up. They walked through the village and across a strip of dried grass to the edge of the withered jungle. Luna stood silently with the other women and watched them go. The sound of the children's voices was clear and bell-like in the evening air. When it was too dark to see the men and the children any more, the women turned silently away and walked to their huts.

The men of the village brought the children to the edge of the jungle and walked twice a hundred paces more. Gradually the dry brown trees and the crackly brush gave way to the moist green of the old jungle. When they had left the blighted area they stopped. The children were taken to the base of a gnarled old tree. The men placed them in a circle with their backs to the tree and had them join hands. Then their wrists were bound with a tough, fibrous vine. Each of the four fathers was charged with seeing that the wrists of his child were securely bound to the next.

Darak knotted the vines that held the wrists of his little boy and was satisfied that they were tight. He glanced back over his shoulder at the dark figures of the other men. When he saw that the Leader was not looking his way, he brushed his lips across the silky hair of his son's head.

"Game, Father?" said the little boy.

"The time of games is over. Now you must be very brave. Sing your song, my little cub."

At a gesture from the Leader the four men stepped back from the tree, leaving their children bound there. The son of Darak sought his father's eyes.

"Sing," Darak told him in a whisper.

Obediently the boy began to sing the lullaby in a piping voice that quavered at first, then grew stronger. One by one the other children took up the song. The men of the village moved silently away from the tree, and soon were lost in the darkness and the night sounds of the jungle.

Lying alone on the pallet she shared with Darak,

Luna heard the distant singing of the children. She fancied she could clearly make out the dear voice of her little boy. Alone in the dark, she allowed the tears to come. They filled her eyes and rolled down her cheeks and made little dark spots on the hard dirt floor.

Luna wanted her man with her at this terrible time, but she knew that could not be. The men of the village would spend this night sitting wakefully around a fire in the clearing. They would be very careful to display no emotion, for to do so was to admit weakness. For a woman it was allowed, especially if she were alone. So the woman Luna sobbed quietly as she listened to the far-off singing of the children.

Then abruptly the little voices were silenced as though sliced off with a blade. Luna sat up on the pallet, her dark eyes staring into the deeper darkness of the night.

Then the screaming started. Screams of fear. One of the little girls first, then the other girl. Next the other little boy. Finally her own baby.

Luna caught her lip between strong white teeth. Blood trickled unheeded down her chin and spotted her breast.

The next sound was worse than the screaming. A gruff, snarling challenge. Then the full-throated roar of a beast about to feed.

The cries of the children became screams of pain. Mercifully, the screams did not last long.

Luna sat in the darkness of her hut, hunched over, her fists clenched and pressed against her ears. She tried to shut out the tearing, gobbling sounds of the beasts as they fed. It seemed a very long time before the night was silent again.

The next day it rained.

In the weeks that followed, the rains came with their old regularity. The watering place filled and the animals came again. The crops sprouted and grew with vigor. At the edge of the jungle the trees revived and spread their lush new foliage toward the village.

The weeks grew into months, and the months stretched into years, and the people of the village lived with peace and plenty. Once again they were a happy people. Most of them.

The woman Luna grew older, but she remained straight and handsome. Her black hair was threaded with gray, and there were lines of sorrow around the eyes and at the corners of her mouth. She was a woman alone now. When it became clear that she would bear no more children Darak took another woman, as was his right. Luna understood. She felt no bitterness. This was the law.

Sometimes in the evening when her work was done Luna would walk alone at the edge of the jungle. At these times she would let her thoughts go back to the way it had been when she and Darak and their little boy were all together. The times had been hard then, with the drought. Often there was not enough to eat, and there was illness in the village, but there were times of happiness too. Luna liked to think about those good times of being together, as she walked among the cool shadows in the evening.

On one such evening, as she bent to inhale the fragrance of a night blossom, a sound reached her from the jungle. A sound like nothing she had ever heard.

She straightened and held her breath, listening.

The sound came to her again. It was like a voice, yet not a voice. A soft rumbling, something between a murmur and a growl. And it was calling to her.

The plains dwellers of Luna's village never went into the jungle without a compelling reason. The jungle was filled with things that could hurt and kill. But on this evening Luna did not hesitate. She walked into the thick growth of the rain forest and picked her way through the heavy brush and tangled vines toward the gentle growling voice that called to her.

She found it under the tree of the sacrifice, the tree where the children were left long ago to appease the dark gods. There by the twisted trunk was a huge shadow shape, darker than the darkness of the night. It sat up on powerful haunches, the broad head erect on ebony shoulders. The glowing yellow eyes looked at her.

Luna faced the animal without fear. She marveled at its grace, even at rest. Its glossy coat shimmered in the fragmented moonlight. The paws, each of them big as a man's two fists, were braced on the ground. The killing claws were sheathed and out of sight. It was a thing of deadly beauty. A black leopard.

The beast's mouth opened and closed once, and again. From the muscular throat came its soft growl. Then, visibly straining, the leopard shaped its mouth so the growl came out in a semblance of human speech. One word.

"Mother."

The eyes of the woman filled again with tears. This time they were not tears of sorrow and loss, but of joy. She took a step toward the big cat and opened her arms to it.

"My son."

With a cry almost like that of a child, the leopard was upon her.

Chapter 1

The big cats moved slowly in single file around the inner perimeter of the cage. Standing in the center of the cage, tall and lean in white whipcord, Phillip Gallier watched them sternly. The procession alternated lion, tiger, lion, tiger. Three of each. The cats padded silently around the man, on their great paws, raising little puffs of dust from the dirt floor with each step. The lions carried their big shaggy heads high, their expressions calm, aloof. The tigers had a fiercer look, but they kept warily out of the way of the lions.

Phillip Gallier looked relaxed, but he was aware of the exact position of each cat moment by moment. He carried a stout three-foot cane by which, with subtle gestures, he directed the actions of the animals. A .38-caliber revolver was holstered on his hip, but it was only a part of the uniform. The crowd expected it, and in the circus you did not disappoint the crowd. Yet no one could remember the gun ever being out of its holster.

As the cats continued their parade, Phillip met the eyes of each and called it by name.

"Ho, Gunner, lift that chin. That's it, that's it. You, Pretty Boy, let me see those teeth. Give us a smile. Ah, magnificent. Come on, Captain, pick up those great clumsy feet of yours. Yes, that's more like it. Walk proud. Murphy, back off, there. Back off, you're crowding Captain. Cowboy, stay in line. Cisco, you stop playing with Cowboy's tail or you'll get yourself in trouble. Everybody, heads up now. Remember who you are. You are the lords of the jungle on two continents.

You're the biggest and the strongest of the flesh eaters. Yes, yes, that's it. Now we're all looking good. Way to go, way to go."

Phillip pointed with the cane and the six cats came to a stop before a row of sturdy pedestals. They ranged from two feet high to taller than a man's head. The cats stood, each before his own pedestal, and watched Phillip alertly.

"Ready?" he said.

Muscles tensed under the cats' tawny hides.

"Up!"

At the sharp command the cats mounted with powerful grace to the platforms atop their pedestals.

"Good. That's very good."

One of the lions slipped a little and teetered on his perch.

"Steady, Captain, you're all right. Steady, boy."

The lion regained his balance, and Phillip surveyed the row of cats as they sat on their platforms, waiting. When he was satisfied that he had their full attention he raised the cane and pointed toward the ceiling.

"Ready? Everybody be tall, now. Stand!"

Obediently the big cats rose, balancing on their hind feet, front paws held out in front of them.

"Good. That's very good. Now let's hear how you can sing."

The great jaws opened and the beasts roared at the ceiling, the sky, the world, and mankind. It was a sound that a man would not forget soon.

"Beautiful," Phillip told them like a pleased choirmaster. "Just beautiful. All right, ready . . . down."

The cats dropped back to all fours and descended easily to the floor of the cage. Phillip gestured with the cane, and they circled the cage single file again and headed one by one through the gate that would take them through the chute to the holding cages. Five of the cats left the big cage without incident, but the last, Gunner, largest of the lions, held back. He turned toward Phillip, showed his teeth, and gave him a rumbling roar. Phillip held out the cane, and Gunner swatted at it with one huge paw. Phillip snatched the cane back. Gunner's blow would have knocked it thirty yards away, or broken the back of a zebra.

Outside the cage Richie Laymon, twenty years old and very nervous, stood holding an eight-foot pole, barbed at the end. Richie knew that this was part of the act, that Gunner always took a swipe at Mr. Gallier on the way out, but the sight of those teeth and that mighty paw never failed to give him gooseflesh.

Richie was thankful that this was not his regular job. During the actual performance Mr. Gallier would be assisted by his wife, Nora, cool and beautiful in her spangled tights. Richie would be back in the center ring doing what he loved the most, clowning. With a big greasepainted smile he could make people laugh— young, old, rich, poor, it didn't matter. It seemed a far more rewarding job to Richie than scaring the socks off people by going into a cage with a bunch of killer cats.

Now, inside the cage, things were not going the way they should. Gunner had moved away from the gate to the chute and was menacing Phillip Gallier as though he meant it. The lion's great shaggy head was down, his tail slashing back and forth. Dangerous signs.

Richie moved uncertainly along the bars outside the cage, not sure just what was expected of him if a real emergency should develop. He wiped the palms of his hands one at a time on his trousers so he could grip the pole better. Phillip signaled him to stand still. The trainer's hand never even moved in the direction of the holstered pistol.

Phillip stood his ground in the cage, with only the useless cane as protection against the lion. As Richie watched through the bars, sweat soaking his shirt, Phillip tossed away the cane. He raised one hand as though in benediction and walked toward the lion. Gunner roared thunderously and raised his paw as though to strike again. The needle-sharp claws slipped out of their sheaths. In a fraction of a second they could strip a man's flesh from breastbone to pubis.

Phillip Gallier did not falter. He walked up to the lion, lowered his hand, and scratched the cat behind one ear. "What's the matter, Gunner? Feeling cranky today? We can't have that. You're my star. I expect you to show the others how to behave."

Looking as embarrassed as it is possible for a cat to look, the lion lowered his paw. He pushed his big head against Phillip's leg for more ear-scratching.

"That's more like it. We don't want people to think there are hard feelings between us."

The lion rumbled deep in his chest.

"That's the boy. Go on out now. We'll give the people a real show this afternoon."

The lion turned away, docile as a puppy now, and ambled out through the gate.

When the cat had disappeared through the chute into the holding cage, Phillip Gallier walked out through the main cage door and joined Richie Laymon. The young man still held the barbed pole in a white-knuckled grip.

"They're feeling frisky today," Phillip said. "We should have a fine show."

Richie swallowed, trying to moisten his throat. "That last one had me a little nervous."

"Gunner? He was just kidding around."

"Kidding? Those claws looked like so many knife blades. Couldn't you have them pulled?"

Phillip's face darkened. "You don't pull a cat's claws. That would be like taking away his manhood."

"If you say so. I'll tell you one thing, though, Mr. Gallier. You couldn't pay me enough to go in there and do what you do."

Phillip relaxed and smiled. His teeth were strong and white in the dark face. "It's got to be in your blood, Richie. Either you're born to the cats or you're not. And if you're not, forget it."

"I'll be glad to," Richie said. He leaned the barbed pole against the bars of the cage and dug into a pocket for a set of keys. "I've got the keys to the pickup if you're ready to go into town now."

"I think I'll let it go until tomorrow," Phillip said. "The concessions all have enough supplies for today's shows. Our licenses are all in order. The local farmers will be here between shows to load the manure. Besides, I'm a little tired. I think I'll catch a quick nap in the trailer before the afternoon show."

Richie frowned. "What about feed for the animals?"

"There's plenty of feed. You know I always take care of that before anything else." He looked more closely at the young man. "Is something bothering you, Richie?"

"No," he said quickly. "Nothing. It's just, well, it's still early and I thought there'd be things for you and me to do in town."

"You go on in if you want to. Take the pickup. I'm going to take advantage of this free time to stretch out for a while."

Richie did not move.

"Something *is* bothering you." Phillip's voice held the same tone of quiet authority as when he talked to the cats.

"No, really, it's nothing." Richie took a quick backward step. "Maybe I will take the truck into town, if it's okay. I'll see you."

The young man walked swiftly away across the fresh sawdust that had been spread on the ground. Phillip

17

watched him go, a small frown line between his eyes. Then he shrugged and walked off in the other direction and out of the tent, toward where the trailers were parked.

He walked past the big trucks—only three of them, it wasn't a large circus. As always, the ornate gilt lettering on the side panels of the trucks gave him a thrill. *Gallier Family Circus.*

Phillip's father had formed the show in the first decade of the century, when the circus was truly a part of American life. Now, more than fifty years later, people would rather stay home and watch television than go out and see live performers and real animals. The circus was a dying form of entertainment. A couple of the big ones played the arenas in the major cities, and only a handful of small shows like the Gallier Family was left for the little towns.

There was not much money in it, but it was the only life Phillip Gallier ever wanted. He loved the crowds and the camaraderie of the circus people. He loved the smells—sawdust, cotton candy, hot dogs, manure. And he loved to watch the tents and the midway booths go up magically at each new town.

Most of all, he loved the cats. Like his father before him, Phillip Gallier had a rapport with the big cats that others found uncanny. He could have named his price to go with Ringling Bros./Barnum & Bailey, but Phillip preferred to work with his own small company, and his own cats. The money he might have made appearing in places like Madison Square Garden meant nothing to him. Here he was in control of his destiny.

He walked past the trucks and into the area set aside for the trailers that housed the circus performers and the traveling crew. Here lived the aerialists, the clowns, the specialty acts, and the concessionaires. His own trailer was the largest. He shared it with Nora and their two children. The Gallier trailer was next to the cat cages.

Phillip paused before turning in to his trailer. Standing in front of the one cat cage that was set apart from the others he saw his children, Paul and Irena. At thirteen Paul was already doing a turn with the tumblers. Phillip was not yet ready to work him with the cats. There was something about the dark-eyed, serious boy that disturbed him. Irena was a laughing, friendly child of four. She was a favorite of the performers and the crew.

Phillip walked down to join his children. They stood without speaking, before the bars of the isolated cage. Irena chewed solemnly on a caramel apple. Paul flexed his fingers nervously. Phillip walked up behind them and stood there silently, watching with them.

Inside the cage, its rich coat glistening like deep water in the moonlight, was the black leopard. The leopard did not perform. He was with the circus for exhibition only. For all their skill, neither Phillip Gallier nor his father had ever trained a black leopard to work with the other cats.

The leopard lay comfortably at the back of the cage, a heavy, gnawed bone on the floor before him. One of the huge black paws rested easily on the other. The cat gazed out at the people with hooded yellow eyes.

"Saying hello to our friend, are you?" Phillip said quietly.

The children turned toward him. Irena impulsively wrapped her arms around his booted leg.

"Oh, Daddy, he's so beautiful," she said. "I wish we could take him in the trailer with us."

Phillip reached down and swept his daughter off her feet. He cradled her easily in the crook of his arm. "I don't think that would be wise."

19

"He's strong too," Paul said, turning back to the leopard. "Stronger than the lions, I bet."

"I don't know about that," Phillip said, "but he's a lot stronger than you or I."

"Do leopards kill people, Daddy?" Irena asked.

"Sometimes," Phillip answered. "If they are starved or mistreated or forced out of their natural home by people, then they may kill."

"Why would anybody want to hurt them?" Irena said. "They're so beautiful."

"I don't know. Men often destroy beautiful things without any reason."

Paul changed the subject. "How come you didn't go into town after you worked the cats?"

"I decided I could use a little rest before the early show. Is your mother in the trailer?"

Both children nodded their heads up and down.

"I guess she's taking a nap too," Paul said.

"She told us to play outside and not bother her," Irena added.

The fine hairs rose at the base of Phillip's neck. "Is she feeling all right?"

"She didn't say anything," Paul offered, "and she looked all right to me."

"Me too," Irena put in.

"Well, I'll just go look in on her," Phillip said.

"Can we come too, Daddy?" Irena asked. "I'm tired of playing outside."

"No." Phillip looked off toward the trailer. It looked dark and somehow ominous, silhouetted against the heavy gray sky of mid-morning. "You kids stay out here for a while. Talk to the leopard."

Phillip left them and walked back toward the trailer that was their home ten months out of the year. Most of the other two months they stayed in a motel near the show's winter quarters, in Florida. There was a big family house in New Orleans, but it stood empty most of the time. Nora would have liked to spend more time there, to join in the bright New Orleans social life, but Phillip could not stand to be separated for long from his beloved cats. As for the children, they thought traveling with the circus was the best of all possible ways to live.

The air had grown heavy by the time Phillip reached the trailer. There was a storm heading this way. Phillip hoped the wind would not be too strong. Wind played havoc with the tents. He pushed open the trailer door and walked in.

The compact living quarters, including the kitchenette and the children's bunks, were empty. Everything was neat and orderly, as Nora always kept it. Three long strides and Phillip was at the hanging curtain that closed off their bedroom. He swept it aside and walked in.

Nora looked up at him from the pillow on her side of the bed. The dark hair framed her face in soft, tangled waves. Her breasts were bare where the sheet was pulled down. She made no attempt to cover them.

Ivan Shoffner, or the Great Samson, as he was billed, leaped from the bed beside Nora and stood pressed against the far wall. He clutched at a blanket, trying to cover his nakedness. His beautifully muscled body gleamed with perspiration. Samson's eyes were huge, the whites showed all around the irises. His gaze bounced between Phillip's face and the gun holstered at his hip.

"Now, Phillip, wait a minute. Don't do anything crazy." The strong man's voice was pitched several tones higher than normal.

"Get out of here, Samson." Phillip's eyes were on his wife.

21

The strong man scrambled for his clothes, which lay on the floor at the foot of the bed. "Right, Phillip, I'm going." He danced around awkwardly on one foot, trying to get the other into his black bikini briefs without taking his eyes off Phillip and the gun.

"Never mind the clothes," Phillip said. "Just get out. Now!" The last word cracked like a whip.

Samson crushed his clothing into a ball and edged out through the curtain, keeping as far as he could from Phillip in the confines of the trailer bedroom. Once he was past the curtain, he fairly leaped from the trailer, banging the door behind him.

Phillip did not look around. He continued to stare down at Nora Gallier.

She licked her lips. Her eyes were bright, but more with excitement than fear.

"Hello, Phillip."

He looked at her for a long moment before he spoke. Then his voice was a rasp. "Why? Why did you do this, Nora?"

"It just happened. Nobody planned it."

"That's a lie. You planned it. You were deliberately careless so I would be sure to find you. Even so, it took me a long time to get here, didn't it? Even young Richie knew about it. How long have you been doing this?"

"Not so long. A month. Six weeks."

"Was there anyone else before this one?"

"No. Samson was the only one."

"Does it make you happy to hurt me, Nora?"

Her eyes grew softer. "It isn't that, Phillip. I never wanted to hurt you. I just wanted to be like other people for a little while. Samson was close, and he was easy, so I took him."

"It was a mistake," Phillip said. "You can never be like other people. Neither can I. You know that. You know what we are. We must always stay with our own kind. You and I and the children."

"It will never happen again, Phillip."

"It *must* never happen again," he said. "Look at you." He whipped the sheet down and off the bed, exposing his wife's body. "It's just a matter of time until Samson stays a few minutes too long and sees you like this. Samson or somebody else. I can't allow that to happen."

Phillip Gallier unsnapped the holster on his hip and drew out the revolver. He stood over the bed and took careful aim. For the last time he looked into the eyes of his wife.

"I love you, Nora," he said, and he pulled the trigger.

The report of the pistol was like a cannon in the little room. The body on the bed jumped convulsively, writhed for a moment in the final agony, then lay still.

"Daddy!"

Phillip turned from the bed and saw his children standing wide-eyed and terrified behind him. Paul was holding the bedroom curtain aside. Irena had her little hands pressed to her mouth.

Phillip took a step toward them.

"I'm sorry, my darlings. I love you both very much, but you should never have been born. I will try to make it as painless as possible for you. Believe me, this will save you from much worse pain later in your lives."

He raised the gun, but for a crucial fraction of a second he could not pull the trigger. In that moment of hesitation Paul seized his little sister, bounded back through the trailer, and dived out the door. Already adept at tumbling, the boy hit the ground, protecting Irena as best he could, rolled, and sprang to his feet. By the time Phillip reached the door, the children were nowhere in sight.

"God help both of you," he muttered. Then he turned

and walked back into the tiny bedroom. He lay down on the bed, put the muzzle of the revolver in his mouth, and blew the top of his head off. They found him there that afternoon, lying beside the dead leopard.

Chapter 2

The DC-10 banked gently over Lake Pontchartrain and began its final approach to the New Orleans International Airport. Irena Gallier watched nervously from the window beside her coach seat, her hands in her lap with the fingers laced tightly together. She was twenty-one years old, and this was her first time in an airplane.

The landing gear hit the runway with a soft thump. The big engines roared as the pilot reversed the thrust. The heavy plane slowed rapidly until it was taxiing along at no more than twenty miles an hour. Irena relaxed. She wiped her palms on a wadded Kleenex.

The chunky redheaded man in the next seat turned a big grin toward her. "There, now, it wasn't all that bad, was it?"

Irena smiled back at him, relieved that her smile came naturally. During the flight the man had told her he was a salesman for a cosmetics firm and that he was returning to his family in New Orleans after an extended selling trip to visit dealers up and down the Eastern Seaboard. Irena knew the man had talked so much to her because she showed her nervousness about flying, but she appreciated it nevertheless.

"It wasn't bad at all," she told him. "I feel foolish now for worrying about it. Thanks for helping to keep my mind off where I was."

"Shoot, it was my pleasure," the salesman said. "I always enjoy having somebody to talk to."

As the jet continued taxiing toward the terminal, Irena took out a small mirror and a hairbrush. Her short, boy-cut dark hair and huge lustrous eyes made her seem even younger than she was.

The plane came to a stop, and there was a general movement toward the exit as the passengers unbuckled and stepped out into the aisles.

The salesman retrieved his topcoat and carry-on bag from the overhead compartment. He gave her a parting smile. "Good luck to you."

"Thanks. You too."

She checked to see that she had left nothing in the pocket on the seat-back in front of her, then stood up and joined the others inching toward the exit.

Once inside the terminal she hung back as, one after another, the deplaning passengers were greeted by people waiting there for them. She wondered if she would recognize her brother, Paul. It had been almost seventeen years since she had seen him.

All around her there was laughter, and a few tears too. People were hugging and kissing and shaking hands, and everybody was smiling. Irena saw the cosmetics salesman greeted by a plump, pretty woman and two energetic redheaded boys. He glanced over toward her, then separated himself for a moment from his family and walked in her direction.

"Is somebody meeting you?" he said.

"Yes, my brother. He lives here. He's probably a few minutes late."

"Probably," the man agreed. "He might be here now, waiting down at the baggage claim. Lots of people wait down there."

"That could be where he is," Irena said. She gave him another smile, but this one was less than genuine. "Thank you."

"Don't mention it. Take care of yourself."

"You too. Goodbye."

She watched the salesman walk back to rejoin his

family. She was relieved to be rid of him, even though all he wanted to do was help. He had made her feel suffocated.

Now, as she watched him slip an arm familiarly around his wife's waist, with the two boys capering along beside him, Irena felt a twinge of envy. Would she ever be a wife, with a husband and a family of her own? Would she ever be free to live a normal life?

The last of the passengers had left the arrival area, and no one had come forward to greet her. Irena began to feel uneasy about standing there alone, as though unseen eyes were watching her. She saw a sign reading "Baggage Claim," with an arrow pointing toward a DOWN escalator. She walked quickly in that direction.

The baggage-claim area was cold and impersonal. It had a concrete floor and a big metal turntable onto which the luggage slid from a chute. The passengers from Irena's flight stood around the perimeter of the turntable waiting to seize their own bags as they rode past.

Irena stood at the rear of the crowd, searching the faces for someone who might be Paul. Finally the people melted away, and there were only a few forlorn pieces of luggage still revolving on the turntable. One of them was the new Weekender she had purchased for this trip. Could Paul have gotten the time of her flight wrong? she wondered. Or mixed up the date? Her nervousness increased.

The next time her bag came around she hoisted it off the turntable and set it down on the floor. She had packed a lot into the bag, and it was heavier than it looked. As she started to pick it up again, a smiling young man strode toward her from the far side of the room. He had a clean-cut, collegiate look. Paul? No, he was too young. Still, he was making directly for her. Irena answered his smile tentatively.

"Hello, there," the young man said. "How are you?"

"All right," Irena said carefully.

"Well, you sure look all right to me, but I guess there's none of us who couldn't be just a little bit better. Am I right?"

Irena did not answer.

"Just because you're all right and I'm all right, I want to make you a present of this book."

For the first time Irena noticed that the young man was carrying a stack of slim green volumes cradled in one arm. He slipped one off the top of the stack and held it out to her.

"Go ahead and take it. It's absolutely free. No obligation. Just a gift from me to you, in the spirit of universal brotherhood."

Irena glanced at the title stamped in gold on the cover: *Achieving Everlasting Peace and Harmony*. "I don't think I can accept it."

"Please," the young man coaxed, continuing to smile. "I told you it's a gift. If you do wish to make a donation, it will go to a good cause, and I can assure you it will be appreciated."

"No, I don't think so."

Irena started to move away from him. The young man danced sideways to block her path. His smile hardened at the edges.

"If you'll just take the time to look through the book, I think you'll be surprised at what you see. It might very well change the entire course of your life, as it has so many others'."

"I'm sorry, I'm not interested. Let me pass, please."

Again she tried to get past the boy, and again he moved to block her way. He was standing uncomfortably close to her.

"Here." He thrust the book at her. "I'm offering it to you free. A gift. Read just a little of what the prophet has to tell us." His manner turned subtly threatening. "Or aren't you interested in the way to find everlasting peace and harmony?"

"Let me pass," Irena told him. "I don't want your book."

The young man moved swiftly and took hold of her elbow. Irena looked around the baggage room for someone she might appeal to for help. The few people in sight were standing well away from them, and were absorbed with their own affairs. There was no one who looked like he might work for the airport. No policeman.

The young man grasped her elbow firmly and raised the stack of books close to her face.

"I don't think you understand," he said. "It's free. You can make any kind of a donation you want to. You have the opportunity to improve your life immeasurably this very afternoon. You're not going to pass up that opportunity, are you? I promise you, you'll regret it."

"Let go of my arm, you're hurting me."

"Just let me show you some of the more meaningful passages in the book." The young man's breath was warm and moist on her face. It smelled of licorice.

"Let her go."

The deep, commanding voice coming from close behind her startled Irena. The boy too looked up, surprised. He quickly released his grip on her arm and stepped back, staring at whoever stood behind her.

Irena turned. She saw a tall man, about thirty, wearing a dark suit and a clerical collar. His eyes were large and dark in a pale face. They flashed now with a dangerous anger.

"I was only offering her a book," the boy said.

"I know what you were doing. I am telling you to leave her alone. *Now.*"

The boy faced the older man for only a moment, then

he spun away and hurried off with his stack of books, through the door leading outside the terminal.

Irena smiled up at the tall man. "Thank you. I wasn't sure what he was going to do."

"Most of them are harmless, but they can be a terrible nuisance." He gestured toward her suitcase. "May I help you with that?"

Irena glanced around uncertainly. "Well, I'm, uh, waiting for my brother. He was supposed to meet me here."

The tall man smiled down at her. "What's the matter, Irena, don't you recognize me?"

She looked at him more closely. "Paul? Is it really Paul?"

"Welcome home, little sister," he said, and opened his arms to her.

Irena hugged him. His cheek was smooth and cool. He had a sharp, clean scent of shaving lotion. His body was surprisingly hard and muscular against hers.

Paul released her abruptly and stepped back. "I'm sorry I wasn't upstairs to meet your flight. I got hung up in traffic."

"That's all right, we're together now." Irena let her eyes run over him. She pointed to the clerical collar. "I didn't know you were a . . . a . . ."

"A man of God?" He laughed. "Actually I'm just a lay minister. I do what I can to help out at the Tabernacle Mission in the French Quarter."

"How did you happen to . . . I mean, how did it come about?"

His eyes grew serious. "For about ten years I lived the kind of a life that I'm really ashamed of now. I just decided one day that it was time I balanced the books." He touched the collar. "If this bothers you I can take it off."

Irena hugged him again. "No, of course not. I think

it's wonderful, and I'm just so glad to see you. We've got so much to talk about."

"Yes, little sister, that we do."

He picked up her heavy suitcase as though it were filled with feathers, circled her waist with his free arm and led her out of the terminal.

Chapter 3

As Paul drove in toward the city, Irena sat forward in her seat, looking around, trying to find something familiar.

"What do you think of the old home town?" Paul asked. "If we can call it that."

"It's like I'm seeing it for the first time."

"That's not surprising. We never did spend a lot of time here, and you were just a toddler the last time the family was all together. Just three years old, I guess."

"The city looks so . . . so new."

Paul laughed. "A lot of it is. Mostly on the north side, or Uptown, as we call it. A lot of new houses there. Then on the river there's the new International Trade Mart. All the big hotel chains have new buildings here—Hilton, Hyatt, Marriott. We also have high-rise apartments and condominiums. Yes, New Orleans has a skyline now."

"I hope they didn't destroy all the old things to make way for the new," Irena said.

"Oh, no, the city is still a mixture of the old and the new. Tomorrow I'll take you on a tour of Downtown and show you some *really* old New Orleans. The Vieux Carré, the Old Square."

"Is that the French Quarter?"

"Right. Founded in 1718 by Sieur de Bienville. I guarantee you'll get your fill of local history there."

"I'll enjoy that." Irena looked off to her right. "What's that huge thing? The one that looks like a grounded flying saucer?"

"That's the Superdome, home of the Sugar Bowl.

Someday we hope to have a professional football team to put in it. Until then we have to make do with the Saints."

Irena looked blank.

"Local joke," Paul explained.

They drove in on broad, busy Canal Street, lined with office buildings and hotels. In minutes they had left the modern, bustling city and were cruising along St. Charles Avenue, between the elegant old houses set back on sweeping lawns. The late-afternoon sun dappled the graceful mansions as it filtered through stately elm trees.

"What a lovely street," Irena said.

"Our house isn't quite as impressive as these," Paul said, "but it's a whole lot better than living in a trailer."

After another mile Paul brought the car to a stop. Across the sidewalk from them was a tall, spiked iron fence. Beyond the fence, partially hidden by untrimmed elm trees, stood a two-story brick house with a pillared portico at the end of a short walk. A balcony with a wrought-iron railing extended across the entire upper floor. The windows Irena could see were clouded. The yard needed tending. The place had a remote, lonely look, as though nobody lived there.

"Does the old place stir any memories?" Paul asked.

Irena shook her head. "I guess I was too young to form memories. It does look like something I've seen in my dreams, though."

"Maybe that's the same thing."

They got out of the car, Paul once again effortlessly lifting the heavy bag. He held the gate for her and they walked through the fence and up the path to the front door.

Paul reached past her and pushed the heavy oak door open. Irena walked in and stood looking around.

The high-ceilinged entrance hall with the filtered sun-light made her think of a cathedral. There was a musty, old smell to the place, and beneath that something else. Something raw.

"What do you think?" Paul said, startling Irena out of her reverie.

"It's ... impressive. You don't live here alone, do you?"

"Oh, no. In fact, sometimes I feel like I'm just a boarder here, the way Femolly takes charge of things."

"Femolly?"

"Unless I'm mistaken, you're about to meet her."

Somewhere in the rear of the big house a door opened and closed. Paul nudged Irena and turned expectantly in that direction. Through the archway leading to the dining room came a tall, regal woman wearing a long, full skirt, a silk blouse, and a colorful scarf on her head. Her skin was a flawless café au lait, her eyes black and shiny. She stopped in front of them, planted her hands on her hips, and examined Irena from head to foot.

"So! Here's the little girl come home at last. Only not so little any more, hah?"

Paul said, "Femolly, this is my sister, Irena."

"Who else could it be?" the tall woman demanded. "With those eyes—those Gallier eyes. You are your mother all over again, child. Only prettier, I think. Yes, definitely prettier."

"Thank you," Irena said, feeling uncomfortable under the woman's scrutiny.

"Femolly doesn't fit the usual image of the faithful family retainer, does she?" Paul said.

Irena smiled but couldn't think of anything to say.

"Just don't let her start bossing you around, or she'll be insufferable."

"Don't you listen to that brother of yours, child,"

Femolly said. "He's just a lot of fancy talk. You should have seen him moping around here the last couple weeks just like a little boy, waiting for his sister to come home where she belong."

Irena smiled at her.

"Don't you worry, child, you and me gonna get along just fine. Won't neither of us take any foolishness from this preacher-man brother of yours."

Femolly made a point of turning a disapproving frown on Paul, but Irena could not miss the deep affection the woman felt for her brother.

"I'm sure we'll do just fine," Irena said.

The tall woman beamed at her.

"Femolly," Irena tried the name experimentally. "I've never heard the name before. Where does it come from?"

"It comes from the state of Louisiana, I guess. See, when I was born my momma died, and there wasn't no daddy around to claim me, so on the birth certificate they just put down Child, Female. Now, the woman who brought me up, rest her soul, she couldn't read English that good, so she thought you said it to rhyme with tamale. So that's who I been ever since. Female . . . Femolly."

"I think it's a beautiful name," Irena said.

"Thank you, child, it's done all right for me. You run along now and wash up. We gonna have us a real New Orleans dinner."

"See what I told you about her getting bossy?" Paul said.

"I don't mind a bit," Irena said. She followed the tall dark woman to the downstairs bathroom.

Femolly served dinner to Paul and Irena, who sat across from each other at one end of the long table in the dining room. Irena wondered idly if the other end of the table were ever used.

The aroma of the food soon chased idle speculations out of her mind. From a heavy china tureen Femolly ladled out steaming plates of thick gumbo with big chunks of white crabmeat and tender oysters in it. For dessert there was a sinfully rich pecan pie with a pot of hot chicory-flavored coffee to wash it all down.

Irena pushed back from the table with a long, contented sigh. "How on earth do you stay so slim with this kind of food?"

"Exercise," Paul said. "I try to run every day. And I ride a bicycle."

"Do you swim?"

Paul's face clouded. "No. I don't like going in the water."

Irena was surprised by his change of mood. "I've never been a swimmer either," she said. "I suppose we'll find a lot of things we have in common."

Paul's good spirits returned. "I wouldn't be surprised. Anyway, we'll have lots of time to learn about each other now. What are your plans?"

"I want to start looking for a job."

"There's no hurry about that, is there?"

"I just feel that after you put me through art school, it's time I started paying my way."

"Don't worry about it," Paul said. "It was something I wanted to do. I wanted to bring you home sooner but, well, there were complications here that prevented me from even coming to see you."

Irena was touched by his sincerity. She reached across the table and pressed his hand. "Never mind, brother, we're together now."

"Yes," he said, "and we've got a lot of catching up to do." He cocked his head and looked at her. "Apparently we both survived the years in foster homes without any serious damage."

"It was never a lot of fun," Irena said, "but we could

have had it a lot worse. I'm just sorry we had to be separated all these years."

"It won't happen again," Paul told her. He looked over at the six-foot grandfather clock tick-tocking sedately in a corner of the room. "I suppose you're tired after the plane ride."

"I am, a little, but I'm much too excited to go to sleep yet."

"There's no rush. We keep pretty liberal hours around here. Come on upstairs and I'll show you your room."

While Femolly cleared away the dinner dishes, Irena followed Paul up the broad stairway to the second floor. Irena slowed to look at the paintings that were hung along the staircase wall. They were strange primeval landscapes of jungles and desert, with misty mountains in the distant background. The paintings were heavy with shadows in which living things seemed to lurk just out of sight.

"Are you coming?" Paul called from up on the landing.

Irena pulled her gaze from the paintings. "Right behind you."

He was waiting for her in front of an open door along a short hall. Irena went past him into a small, immaculate room. There was a wardrobe chest and a bureau with plenty of drawer space. A big window looked out on the balcony at the front of the house. A fresh breeze stirred the white gauze curtains.

"I love it," Irena said.

"You'll probably want to decorate it to your own taste once you're moved in. Feel free to make any changes you want."

"Paul, I'm not sure I'll be staying here that long," she said.

The shadow crossed his face again. "Not staying here? What do you mean? This is your house as much as it is mine."

"It's just that I might want a place of my own. A little apartment, maybe. This house is so big."

Paul dismissed the subject with a wave of his hand. "There'll be plenty of time to talk about it." They walked back into the hall together. "My room is two doors down, on the other side of the bathroom. Now, since you're not ready to go to bed, I want to show you the playroom."

"Playroom?" Irena repeated.

"That's what I call it." Paul started toward the rear of the upper story. "Come on, I think you'll enjoy this."

He led her into a large, high-ceilinged room that was lit more brightly than the rest of the house. The walls were covered with wildly colored circus posters in styles that ranged from the early years of the century to the mid-1960s. Hanging from wall hooks were glittery circus costumes and clown suits. Everywhere there was circus memorabilia—an antique popcorn machine, the garish front of an old ticket booth, a side-show banner featuring a bearded lady, a lion tamer's whip, a pedestal for a performing animal, a wire-walker's parasol.

"Isn't this something?" Paul said.

Irena gazed around the room in wonder. "How did you ever get all these things together?"

"When I was old enough to move back here into the house I wrote all over the country asking people who might know what happened to the old Gallier Family Circus equipment. After Mother and Dad died all of it was sold off to pay the bills. Most of it is gone forever, of course, but whenever I could trace down a piece from the circus I'd buy it and have it shipped back here. For this room. I think the folks would have liked it." He broke off and looked at Irena sharply. "You don't mind my talking about them, do you?"

"No, it's all right. I know all about how they died, but

I don't remember it. I suppose you'd call it a psychological block."

"I'd call it a blessing," Paul said. He looked around the room, his eyes glowing. "I really love it. The circus, I mean. I was training to be a performer, you know."

"No, I didn't."

"Oh, yes."

Without changing his expression, Paul suddenly flipped over backwards. Irena gasped in surprise. He hit the floor with the flat of his hands, flexed, and bounced catlike back to his feet. He grinned at her boyishly.

Irena laughed and clapped her hands. "That's wonderful."

"I think I would have made a pretty fair acrobat, don't you?"

"If that's an example, you'd have been terrific," Irena said.

"Oh, I have lots of other tricks, but I'll save them. There's no sense doing the whole show out in front, as Dad used to say."

Irena picked up a photo album from a table along one wall. It fell open to a picture of a handsome young couple—the man in whipcord breeches and boots, the woman in spangled tights. Irena showed the picture to Paul. "Is this our mother and father?"

"Yes. Notice how much they look like us?"

Irena studied the photograph. It was true, especially around the eyes. Allowing for differences in hair style and makeup over the past twenty years, the Phillip and Nora Gallier in the picture could have been their own son and daughter.

Irena flipped past several pages. She stopped at a faded old photo from which a heavy-browed man with a luxurious moustache gazed out at her with the dark Gallier eyes.

"This must be Grandfather," she said.

Paul nodded. "Henry Gallier. That picture was taken around 1910 when he started the circus. Even at its peak it was never what you'd call a big show, but Grandfather really started small. One wagon, an elephant that had seen better days, a couple of clowns who doubled as roustabouts. Oh yes, and one cat."

Paul reached out and flipped over the album page. Irena stared at the photo of a huge black leopard. Its fangs were bared, its golden eyes held her hypnotically. When she looked up she saw Paul waiting for her reaction.

"Fierce-looking creature," she said.

"Of all cats, the black leopard is the most difficult to tame," Paul told her.

He held Irena's eyes for a long moment. Finally she turned away, trying to make it casual.

"I think I'm ready to go to bed now," she said.

"If you want anything, you know where I am," Paul said. "Just pound on the door."

"Thank you, Paul." She kissed him lightly on the cheek.

He held her for a moment. Irena could feel the heat of his hands on her back, through the material of her dress. It made her vaguely uncomfortable.

As though he sensed her uneasiness, Paul stepped back and smiled at her easily. "Good night, little sister. I'm glad you're home."

"Good night, Paul," she said. "I'm glad too."

Irena went to her room and found she was even more tired than she thought. She took a nightie from her suitcase, and decided to save the rest of the unpacking until tomorrow. She climbed into bed and sank gratefully into the yielding mattress.

But she did not sleep. The creaks and groans and

sighs of the old house were foreign to her ears, and had to be identified one by one. Outside her window the branch of an elm tree rustled against the iron bars of the balcony railing.

Finally she dozed off, but almost immediately sat up, wide awake. She had an overpowering sensation of being watched. The room was totally black, with the window a faint gray rectangle over the foot of the bed. Squinting, it seemed she could see a shadow there that was darker than the surrounding night.

"Who's there?" she called.

There was no answer.

Did the shadow move?

Irena fumbled for the lamp that stood on the bedside table. She found it and switched it on, flooding the room with light. Nothing lurked outside the window except the gently waving branch of the elm tree.

Irena put out the light and lay back down. Nerves, she told herself. It had been a long, eventful day. Nothing was out there watching her. Still, it was a long time before she fell into a fitful sleep.

Chapter 4

It was late, and Ruthie Warren was tired.

Too much time on my feet today, she thought with grim humor, and not enough on my back.

She paused on her way down Bourbon Street to look into the window of an X-rated bookstore. There was a heavy crimson drapery behind the glass to give the customers inside a measure of privacy while they browsed among the fleshy magazines. It also provided a good reflection for people passing on the street.

Ruthie frowned at the image that looked back at her. Christ, she was showing all of her twenty-nine years tonight. All right, then, her thirty-three years. Hooking was a young girl's profession. What she dreamed of was latching on to some well-fixed john who would put her up in a little pad of her own and give her spending money. Not a whole lot, just enough to buy little things now and then.

The whore's dream, she thought bitterly. Fat chance of it ever coming true. Definitely not taking calls from the crummy massage parlors on Bourbon Street. When Eddie Mays had called her tonight she felt like telling him where he could stick his business. But face it, she could use the extra bread.

Ruthie patted her Farrah Fawcett wig, turned away from the window, and click-clacked on up the street on her spike heels. The tourist crowd was way off tonight. There was no convention in town, nothing going on in the Superdome. Just a lot of kids looking to score some dope, and the usual well-dressed Japanese who took pictures of everything in sight but didn't buy much.

At the corner of Conti Street she passed the New Original Dixie Bar. Inside the open door four ancient black men honked out a brand of jazz that was even older than they were. Their faces were empty of expression, their thoughts somewhere far away. The tourists inside didn't care. They drank their hurricanes and their pernod and stomped their feet in time with the creaky Dixieland music as though it were being invented on the spot.

Ruthie hurried on past two more bars, a pawn shop, and a hole-in-the-wall theater playing *Deep Throat*. She stopped at a six-foot street-level sign that read: *Pleasure Dome Massage Parlor 1 Flight Up—Satisfaction Guaranteed—Special French & Oriental Body Massage.* Then, in case anyone still did not get the message: *Private Rooms Available—Young Attractive Girls!!!*

Two motorcycle types wearing denim jackets with the sleeves cut off to show their tattoos lounged in the doorway. They passed a marijuana cigarette back and forth and stared hard at Ruthie. One of them broke into a moronic giggle. Ruthie squeezed by without looking at them and climbed the gritty flight of stairs that led to the Pleasure Dome.

At the top of the stairs was a small lobby lit with red bulbs and smelling of strawberry incense. Eddie Mays sat on a stool behind a high counter with a glass front. Behind the glass was a selection of dildoes, handcuffs, rubber mouths, vibrators, French ticklers, and other items advertised as "marital aids" to satisfy the municipal code. Eddie was a sour, thirtyish man with a complexion problem.

"You're late," he said. "It's lucky this john is patient. He's been in there forty-five minutes."

"I got here as quick as I could," Ruthie said. "I wasn't planning to work any more tonight."

"If you don't want these calls, there's plenty of other girls hot to trot."

"I want the calls, Eddie," she said. "I do the best I can."

"Well get on in there and service the guy. It's room twelve."

Ruthie walked down the dimly lit hallway. She stopped at the linen closet to take out a couple of clean towels. Soft rock music was playing over the tinny speakers Eddie had installed. She walked on to a pink-painted door marked *12*. The *2* was missing, but the number was clearly outlined in brighter paint where it had hung. She touched her wig to make sure it hadn't slipped, licked her lips, put on a sexy smile, and walked in.

"Hi, sorry I'm la—"

She stopped just inside the door and looked around. There was the bed, cheap bureau with a mirror, single chair, and nobody. What a hell of a note, she thought, if she came all the way down here for nothing.

Then she saw a man's dark suit neatly folded on the chair. The door to the tiny bathroom was closed, and a seam of light showed along the bottom. Okay, so the john was modest.

She walked over and tapped on the bathroom door. "Ruthie's here, honey. You can come out any time you're ready."

No answer.

Ruthie sighed. She hoped this john was not going to be one of those who had to be coaxed. They knew what they came in here for. Why didn't they just get to it?

She skinned the dress off over her head and held it in one hand while she reached down and took off her shoes with the other. It felt good to get out of the tight pumps.

"Did they fill you in on the prices?" she said to the

44

bathroom door. "The straight massage is twenty-five dollars. I mean, for twenty-five dollars you get a massage and that's it. Tipping is allowed if you want any extras or personal services, if you know what I mean."

The guy had damn well *better* want some extra personal services, Ruthie thought. It would really be a bummer if she had left a comfortable chair and a good movie on TV, squeezed her swollen feet back into shoes, and traipsed all the way down here to Bourbon Street for some yoyo who only wanted a *massage*. She had heard of that happening to other girls.

As she laid her dress across the back of the chair Ruthie saw the bulge of a wallet in the back pocket of the man's folded pants. With a glance at the still-closed bathroom door, she slipped it out deftly and opened it up as she continued to talk.

"For the straight massage you get ten minutes. The extras depend on how complicated you want to get."

The wallet contained a thick, unorganized sheaf of bills. Oddly, there was no identification. What the hell, it was fine with her if the guy wanted to travel incognito. She slipped out a twenty-dollar bill and tucked it into her purse, then replaced the wallet.

"We honor all the major credit cards—Visa, Master Card, American Express, but they're good for the massage only."

She heard a soft scraping sound and quickly smoothed out the man's pants where they lay.

"Tips are strictly on a cash basis."

She unhooked her bra and draped it over the top of her dress. Watching herself in the mirror, Ruthie moved her shoulders to make her breasts swing. Recently she had been thinking about getting silicon implants. They said the process was perfectly safe now. It could be done in the doctor's office. Ruthie studied herself criti-

45

cally and decided the boobs were still plenty good. Time enough to think about implants later.

She sat down on the bed and ran her hands down along her legs. They were her best feature. Her thighs felt warm and resilient under the black nylon stockings. She would leave the stockings and the garter belt on for now. A lot of men found that a turn-on.

She stood up and patted her stomach. A little rounder than she would have liked, but firm.

"Come on out, honey," she called. "We've already used up five minutes of your time."

She started to peel the blanket back off the bed, but stopped when her fingers touched something cold and moist. She straightened a fold in the blanket to look more closely and uncovered a lump of pinkish membrane, something like a piece of uncooked chicken flesh.

Yuck, was this guy going to turn out to be a weirdo? She prodded the lump with a stiff forefinger and shuddered at the slimy feel of it. What the fuck did the guy have in mind? She moved the thing, and beneath it was a pool of bloody mucus. A trail of the stuff, like some obscene snail track, led across the blanket and dripped down into a shiny clot on the floor.

Disgusted yet fascinated, Ruthie leaned down to look at the mess. Something else was down there. Thick and dark, looking like a length of wet black rope, it stuck out from under the bed.

Right then Ruthie decided that whatever this guy wanted, he wasn't going to get it from her. She nudged the black rope with her foot.

It moved.

Ruthie sprang off the bed as though it were electrified. She stared at the wet black thing that now flicked slowly back and forth.

Something in the room growled.

"Jesus and Mary!"

Ruthie began snatching up her clothes as the growl came again, deep and menacing.

The narrow bed shuddered and began to tilt as though something under it were trying to stand up. Something huge and powerful.

Whimpering, Ruthie forgot about her clothes and made a dash for the door. She had her hand on the knob when the bed went over with a crash.

"Oh my God, my God!"

Something grabbed her stockinged foot and pulled her back into the room.

Ruthie screamed in pain and terror. Don't look back at it, she told herself, or it will never let you go. She lunged for the door, with her foot still held fast. She caught hold of the slippery doorknob and fought to make it turn. There was the crunch of bone and a pop as her Achilles tendon gave way under the growling assault of the thing that held her.

At last the doorknob turned in her hand. The door swung open and Ruthie stumbled through it. In the hallway she almost fell into the arms of a frightened Eddie Mays. She slammed the door behind her. Something heavy thumped against it from the other side. There was a growl that rose to a roar of fury.

"What the fuck—" Eddie began.

"Get me out of here!" Ruthie screamed.

With his eyes bulging from the effort, Eddie half-dragged, half-carried Ruthie back along the hallway toward the stairs.

When they came abreast of the counter where Eddie sat, Ruthie looked down at her foot. The front of it was gone—all the toes, the ball of her foot, leaving only a bloody stump of heel. The ankle was ripped open, exposing shattered bone and tendon. Ruthie screamed once more, then she fainted.

Chapter 5

In a small house on Burgundy Street, just over two miles from the Pleasure Dome Massage Parlor, Oliver Yates peered intently down into a glass case. His attention was totally absorbed by an evil-looking gila monster that was crawling lethargically across the sand that covered the bottom of the case.

"I think he's going to be all right," Oliver said, without turning to look at the girl sitting on the couch across the room. "He's showing more life tonight than he did yesterday. If he continues to show improvement, I think we'll have old Tyrone back on display by the first of next week."

"Glad to hear it," said Alice Moore. She made no effort to keep the boredom out of her voice. Alice was a redhead with dazzling green eyes, and a generous mouth that looked great when she laughed. Alice was not laughing now.

Oliver turned away from the big lizard at last and looked at her. "Hey, don't let your enthusiasm run away with you."

She got up and came over to where he was standing and planted a kiss on his cheek. "Believe me, Oliver, I'm really glad that Tyrone is feeling better. I just wish that sometimes you'd look at me with the same concern you show for him."

Oliver started to say something, but Alice went on.

"I know a lot of men take work home from the office with them, but a briefcase full of papers isn't as visible as . . . as one of those."

"It's your work too," he said.

"I know, and it is an honor being chief assistant to one of the youngest zoo curators in the country. I just think it would be nice if the young curator could tear himself away from the four-footed friends long enough to notice that one of his two-footed friends has a new hairdo."

"I noticed, and it's beautiful." Oliver grinned at her.

"Mr. Andrew told me it's almost impossible to mess it up. Why don't we try it out?"

"A heck of an idea," Oliver said. He put his arms around her and drew her in close. They were just getting well into the kiss when the old iron knocker on the front door sounded its clank-clank-clank.

"Damn, who could that be?" Oliver wondered.

"If it's the aardvark with a sore throat, I'm leaving," Alice said.

Oliver gave her an I-can't-do-any-thing-about-it shrug and crossed the living room to open the door.

A broad-shouldered black man in a three-piece suit stood outside under the coach light. Behind him in the street a blue and white New Orleans Police car idled, the lights blinking on its roof bar.

"Dr. Yates?" the man asked.

"I'm Oliver Yates."

"I'm Sergeant George Brant, New Orleans P.D." He held out his wallet to display the shield of the city police and his picture. "May I come in?"

Oliver moved aside and the policeman stepped into the cozy living room. He nodded to Alice, who was still standing by the glass case with the gila monster inside.

"What can I do for you, Sergeant?" Oliver asked.

"I think we might have one of your cats down at the Pleasure Dome Massage Parlor."

Oliver stepped back and looked at him. "This isn't a joke, is it?"

"I'm a policeman on duty, Dr. Yates. I don't make jokes."

"Right." Oliver cleared his throat. "One of my cats, you say."

"We've about narrowed it down to you. All the cats at Audubon are accounted for, there's no circus or wild animal show playing within two hundred miles, and citizens don't keep these babies as pets."

"As of six o'clock this evening no cats had escaped from our zoo," Oliver said. "What kind is it?"

"It's big and it's black, and it looks mean as hell," Brant said. "That's as much as I could see, looking through a peephole into the room where it's holed up."

"Black leopard," Oliver said.

"Whatever."

"That's very strange," Oliver said, looking over at Alice.

"Oh, I don't know," said Brant. "That thing like to tore off a woman's foot, and I'm not about to go into that room, read him his rights, and snap the cuffs on him."

"No, I didn't mean that," Oliver said quickly. "I mean it's strange because the New Orleans Zoo doesn't have a black leopard. We're a pretty small operation, you know, compared to the Audubon."

"As far as I'm concerned, you get that cat out of the Pleasure Dome and your zoo has its leopard. I've got a feeling nobody's going to claim it.'

"I'll be glad to do what I can," Oliver said. "Is this massage parlor on Bourbon Street?"

"Where else?"

"This is my assistant, Alice Moore. If you'll give me the address, we can be there in fifteen minutes."

"I've got a car right outside. I can run you down."

"I'll need my truck," Oliver said. "I have to pick up

some equipment and another man. It shouldn't take me long."

The sergeant shrugged his massive shoulders. "Take your time. That pussycat isn't going anywhere, and I can guarantee you nobody is going in after him before you get there."

He wrote down the address of the Pleasure Dome on the back of one of his cards, handed it to Oliver, and walked back out to the waiting car.

A few minutes later Alice sat in the cab of Oliver's truck outside a peeling stucco apartment house. Oliver came out of the building, walked to the back of the truck, and rechecked the assortment of animal-handling equipment they had picked up at the zoo. He rattled the door on the sturdy steel cage they had brought along, then walked to the front and got in behind the wheel. His eyes shone with excitement.

"Is Joe coming?" Alice asked.

"He wasn't too happy about it, but he'll be along in a minute."

"I wish we didn't have to take him. I don't think he's really comfortable working with animals."

"Joe's still learning," Oliver said. "He's strong, and we might need his help in handling the leopard. I'd a lot rather have one man too many than one too few."

"I suppose so," Alice said, but she did not sound convinced.

The apartment door opened and Joe Creigh came out, tucking a plaid shirt into the waistband of a tight pair of Levis. His lank blond hair fell damply across his forehead.

He pulled open the truck door and climbed in on the other side of Alice. "This is a hell of a time to go out chasing some freaking cat. I hope there's going to be overtime."

"I'll turn in the request," Oliver said, "but don't start

spending it yet. You know how they are about the budget."

"Don't I! Those freaking animals eat better than the help does."

Oliver shot the truck into gear and headed for the French Quarter.

A fair-sized crowd had gathered in the block of Bourbon Street where the Pleasure Dome was. Two police cars and a city emergency truck sat out in front with their lights blinking. Half a dozen uniformed policemen were busy steering the curious away from the entrance to the building. Up the street the musicians in the New Original Dixie Bar honked on.

As Oliver cruised up the block one of the policemen came over and put a hand on the window sill. "This street is blocked off. You'll have to go around."

"I'm Oliver Yates, from the New Orleans Zoo. Sergeant Brant asked me to come down."

"Oh, right." The policeman removed his hand. "Sergeant Brant is waiting for you upstairs."

Oliver left the truck with some satisfaction in a "No Parking" zone and crossed the sidewalk to the entrance. Alice and Joe followed. They climbed the stairs, now bright with police floodlights, to the lobby of the massage parlor. Eddie Mays was sitting in a chair, perspiring heavily, while he answered questions for policemen. Sergeant Brant saw Oliver and beckoned him over.

"Anything new?" Oliver asked.

Brant shook his head. "Status quo. The cat's still locked in the room, and the innkeeper, here, is having a little trouble trying to remember the events of the evening."

Eddie said, "I am telling you everything I know. It beats the shit out of me how that animal got in here."

"You're sure he didn't come up the stairs and slip past you?" said one of the policemen.

52

"Are you kidding? I may not have the eyes of an eagle, but there is no way, *no way* I am not going to see a fucking black panther stroll up my stairs, past my counter, and go into one of my rooms."

"Leopard," Oliver said.

Eddie looked at him for the first time. "What?"

"Black leopard is the correct name for the animal. Not black panther."

"Leopard, panther, what the fuck difference does it make? I know it ain't no chipmunk. Who are you?"

Oliver introduced himself. "Is there a back door to this place?"

"Yeah, but it's always double-locked. It was locked all night. I checked."

"Fire escape?"

"There isn't any." Eddie glanced nervously at Sergeant Brant. "I know I was supposed to put one in, but I was going to apply to the Safety Commission for an extension."

"I don't care about that," Brant told him.

Oliver said, "Do you suppose we could have a look at the cat?"

As though in response to his words, a rumbling growl sounded down the hall from behind the door to room 12.

"Jee*zus!*" Joe Creigh said. "I don't like the sound of that."

"Do you think *I* do?" Eddie complained. "And what about the john who was in the room? He must of been so shook up he took off stark-naked during all the uproar."

Eddie led the party down the hall to a narrow unnumbered room next to room 12. Along both side walls were rows of fish-eye peepholes, separated by shallow plywood partitions to give a semblance of privacy.

"What's this, the voyeur room?" Alice asked.

"It takes all kinds, lady. Some people get their rocks watching somebody else doing it. I make no judgments."

Oliver, Joe, Alice, and Sergeant Brant each put an eye to one of the peepholes on the wall adjacent to room 12. There was a splashy trail of blood in there, from the bed to the door, and some kind of mess on the bed. No animal was in sight.

"Where is he?" Joe asked.

"Under the bed, maybe," Eddie suggested.

"Is it possible he got out the window?" Oliver asked.

"No way. Them bars would hold King Kong."

"What's outside it?"

"Back alley."

Suddenly the bed seemed to explode into the air. A huge black shape sprang at the wall with the concealed viewers. The leopard slashed at it with bloody claws, as though he knew he was being watched from the other side. Reflexively all four of the people at the viewers jerked back from the wall.

"Holy shit!" said Joe.

"He's enormous!" Alice said.

Eddie Mays stood back with his arms folded and looked smug. "What'd I tell you?"

Oliver and Sergeant Brant returned to the viewers.

"He must go hundred seventy, hundred eighty pounds," the detective said.

"Closer to two hundred," Oliver said. "He is a beauty. A real beauty."

"If you can call a nightmare beautiful," Alice remarked.

"So how about getting him the hell out of my place?" Eddie said.

Oliver turned to Alice and Joe. "I'll need some equipment from the truck."

"How about the Winchester twelve-gauge with Mag shells of double-O pellets?" Joe suggested.

54

"I want to capture the cat, Joe," Oliver said patiently, "not blow him to pieces. Bring up the tranquilizer rifle."

"What kind of a load?" Alice asked.

"We'll go with the ketamine straight. Two thousand milligrams. That ought to knock him down fairly quickly so we can get him in the squeeze cage. Better be ready to intubate him too, to keep him breathing."

Alice and Joe hurried out of the room. Their footsteps could be heard clumping down the stairs to the street. Sergeant Brant took another look through the viewer and turned to Oliver.

"Where do you plan to shoot him from?"

"I don't want any holes chopped in my walls," Eddie said. The detective gave him a heavy look, and he fell silent.

"I think the window is our best bet," Oliver said. "Have you got a ladder available?"

"They'll have one on the disaster wagon. You going to want some kind of backup?"

"There isn't much you can do, but thanks."

Oliver took a final look through the viewer to judge the angle his shot would have to take from the window. The leopard stared back at him.

"I have the creepiest feeling that he knows what I'm planning to do," Oliver said, stepping away from the wall.

"Tell you the truth, I'd rather face an armed bank robber," Brant said.

They went downstairs and walked around to the narrow alley that ran behind the building. Brant dispatched men to seal it off at both ends of the block.

The driver of the emergency truck came back with two men carrying an old wooden extension ladder.

"Sorry we haven't got an aluminum model," he said, "but the city cut our budget again."

"I know how you feel," Oliver said.

The ladder was leaned up against the brick wall below the barred window. The two city employees held it steady at the base.

Oliver took the heavy tranquilizer rifle from Joe Creigh.

"Loaded?"

"Two darts," Alice said. "Two thousand mg's of ketamine in each one. From the looks of that animal, you'd better put the first dart in a good spot."

"I intend to," Oliver said. He started up the ladder, then turned back to give her a grin that showed more confidence than he felt.

As he climbed close to the window, Oliver looked down and saw the spear points of an iron fence directly below him. If he fell now, he'd be impaled like an anchovy on an hors d'oeuvres tray. He pushed the image out of his mind and inched upward.

He came even with the bottom of the grillwork and eased his head up over the sill. The accumulated grime on the glass was so thick he could not see into the room. He propped the hand holding the rifle against the brick wall for balance and dug into his pocket for a handkerchief. He reached in carefully through the bars and used the handkerchief to rub at the glass.

Gradually he wiped away enough of the dirt to give him a cloudy view of the interior of the room. He leaned closer to the glass to peer through.

Directly across the room from him the leopard rested on its haunches, looking back at him.

"You were waiting for me, weren't you, boy?" Oliver said. "You just be a good cat and sit right where you are, and this will all be over before you know it."

Moving slowly and awkwardly, careful to maintain his balance, Oliver brought the rifle around in front of him. Gripping it with both hands, he pulled it back so the muzzle was about a foot from the glass, then he thrust it forward. The gun barrel made a solid clunk against the pane, but the window did not break.

"Damn," Oliver muttered.

Inside the room the leopard crouched, tensing his muscles. Through the patch of glass he had cleared, Oliver could see the clear yellow eyes watching him.

"Just take it easy, big fella," he said. "Everything's going to be all right in a few minutes." As an afterthought he whispered, "I hope."

He shoved the muzzle of the rifle against the pane of glass again. Again it bounced off with no effect. Oliver teetered for a moment, pushed off balance by the rebound. Clutching the rifle with one hand, he hugged the wooden upright of the ladder with the other. Someone was shouting down below in the alley, but Oliver ignored it.

He ground his teeth and talked to himself under his breath. "Okay, Superman, all you have to do is break a pane of glass and put a dart into that cat. How will it look if you have to climb back down the ladder and ask for help?"

As he steeled himself to have another go at the window, the leopard sprang. Its two huge forepaws hit the window, and the glass exploded outward as though a bomb had gone off inside.

Oliver clung desperately to the quaking ladder as the leopard slashed at him through the bars. The beast's claws, like deadly curved daggers, gouged strips of wood effortlessly from the ladder. Oliver heard the tough denim of his pant leg rip away as a claw caught it at the knee. A horrified glance down told him that the flesh was not broken.

Again and again the leopard attacked the bars while Oliver struggled to stay out of the way while still holding onto the ladder. Unbelievably, the wrought-iron grillwork over the window began to bend under the assault. The masonry bolts holding the bars to the wall of the building began to work loose. Brick and mortar dust sifted down into the night.

"Good Christ," Oliver thought, "he's coming through!"

"Come down!" a policeman shouted from below him in the alley.

Oliver looked back over his shoulder and saw that one of them was holding a deer rifle.

"Get out of the way and we'll kill him when he shows at the window," the policeman shouted.

"Like hell you will," Oliver said to himself.

He pulled himself back, directly in front of the window. Most of the glass was gone now, and the bars were bent, so he could see clearly into the room. Against the opposite wall the big cat tensed for another attack.

"It's now or never, my friend," Oliver muttered. He brought the tranquilizer gun into position, took hasty aim, and fired.

The recoil knocked him back on the ladder for a moment, but he quickly regained his handhold and leaned forward to look into the room. He saw the dart embedded in the leopard's flank, and breathed a silent prayer. It was a good placement. Lucky.

The cat did not go down at once. It snarled in rage, spinning in circles as it tried to bite at the dart. Then suddenly it stopped and glared at Oliver.

"Don't fight it, big fella," Oliver said. "Just lie down and take a nice little nap."

The leopard launched itself at the window again, but this time the impact lacked force. The animal's strength was ebbing fast as the powerful tranquilizer spread through its body.

"Easy, boy, easy. Don't hurt yourself."

The cat gazed up at him. As though it understood that further efforts to escape were useless, it took out its fury on the room, ripping the bed to ribbons, splintering the chair and bureau, gouging ragged furrows in the plaster walls. Gradually the cat's rage subsided. It sank into a sitting position. The yellow eyes clouded as the beast looked up at Oliver through the shattered window. It bared its fangs in a last show of defiance, then toppled over and lay panting on its side.

Oliver watched for a moment longer, then clambered down the ladder to where a small crowd waited for him in the alley.

"Did you get him?" asked Sergeant Brant.

"I got him," Oliver said, "but I'm not sure how long that dose is going to keep this one down." He signaled to Alice and Joe. "Let's get him into the cage in a hurry. I want to be sure this baby is secure when he wakes up."

Chapter 6

Irena sat up suddenly in bed, her throat constricted, her heart beating wildly. She was gripped by the terror of not knowing where she was or how she got there. It was several seconds before time and place came into synchronization in her mind.

She was in the old Gallier house in New Orleans, in the bedroom given to her by her brother, Paul. She breathed deeply as the terror slowly drained away.

A soft breeze stirred the curtains over the wide window. Outside, over the iron balcony railing, a heavy tree branch bobbed gently up and down. The open window reminded Irena of her dream, in which something that was not quite human had crouched out there, watching her.

She got out of bed and padded barefoot across the hardwood floor to the window. She held the curtain aside and looked out. There was nothing out there but the empty balcony.

Irena let the curtains fall back into place with an exasperated sigh. What had she expected to find, anyway? A bloody footprint or something?

She dismissed the notion and set about unpacking her suitcase. She took out her clothes, a piece at a time, and shook out the travel wrinkles. The smaller things she refolded and placed in the bureau drawers, the larger she hung in the wardrobe chest. When everything was put away to her satisfaction she picked up her little cosmetics bag and stepped out into the hall.

The big house was silent. Irena glanced up and down the hall, saw that all the other doors were closed. She walked to the bathroom, tapped lightly on the door, and when there was no answer she went in.

There were modern fixtures that had obviously been added after the house was built. The smaller bathroom downstairs must have been the original one.

She took a long, luxurious shower and dried herself with one of the fluffy towels hanging on a rod. Her hair was short enough that she would not have to worry about it. It would dry in a few minutes by itself and fall naturally into place.

After wiping down the tub with a sponge, Irena pulled her nightie back on and went back to her room. There was still no one else stirring in the house. What time, she wondered, did people get up here? She took her wrist watch from the bedside table, wound it, and saw that it was nine o'clock. Curious, she pulled on a light nylon robe and went back into the hall. There was still no sound from any other part of the house.

She walked down the hall to Paul's room and rapped lightly on the door.

"Paul?"

She rapped again, more loudly. Still there was no response from inside.

She tried the knob, feeling like a sneak thief. But that was silly, she told herself. Paul was her brother. The knob turned easily in her hand, and the door swung inward.

The big bed, its tall headboard flush against the wall, dominated the room. The bedspread was stretched smoothly across it, the pillows rolled and tucked under. If anyone had slept in the bed last night, he had done a careful job of making it this morning.

Irena stepped tentatively into the bedroom. There was a tang of man's cologne in the air. She walked to the open window and looked out. It gave on the same long balcony that ran outside her room. The trees sighed and whispered in the wind.

Feeling a sudden chill, Irena turned away from the window. She half-expected someone to be standing behind her, but the room was still empty. It was almost bare of furnishings. The only picture on the wall was one of their parents in costume. Each of them was smiling, with an arm extended, palm up, the traditional circus salute to the crowd.

The few personal items in the room—hairbrush, manicure kit, deodorant, talc—were set out on the bureau with geometrical precision. Feeling more than ever like an intruder, Irena backed out of her brother's room, closed the door, and returned to her own.

She dressed quickly, feeling uncomfortably alone in the big house. She was a little annoyed with Paul for not being here when she awoke. He had seemed so warm and glad to see her the day before.

When she went back into the hall she caught the welcome aroma of coffee brewing downstairs. At least she hadn't been completely deserted. Eager for the sound of another human voice, she hurried down.

The kitchen was the warmest, brightest room in the Gallier house. The sun spilled in through a wide window over the sink. Merry pink and red geraniums grew just outside in a window box. One entire wall was hung with well-used pots and pans and cutting implements. Jars, bottles, and cannisters holding mysterious condiments ranged along the counter. The smell of coffee and bacon frying was heavenly.

Femolly stood before a big gas range, tending to a black frying pan. An old-fashioned percolator bubbled gently on a side burner.

"Good morning," Irena said.

"What you want for breakfast?" the dark woman asked. "Eggs or pancakes?"

62

"Eggs will be fine."

"Good thing. I got no pancakes." Femolly turned from the stove with a smile, to show that this was a favorite joke. "All the same, I like to give people a choice."

Irena smiled back at her. She liked this woman, and she liked this room. At the far end of the kitchen was a sturdy round table covered with a red-and-white checkered cloth. On it were a sugar bowl, cream pitcher, and a heavy pair of salt and pepper shakers. Irena started toward it.

"May I set the table?" she asked.

" 'Course not. You don't eat in here, child." Femolly jerked a thumb toward the door leading to the dining room. "You eat out there."

"But this is so much more cheerful."

"You eat out there," Femolly said with finality. "You're not help, you're family. Go 'long now, and I'll bring your breakfast out when it's ready."

Irena sighed and walked out to the dining room. She flicked up the wall switch, but even the lights from the ornate chandelier over the table could not brighten the room's dark woodwork and somber wallpaper. It had been gloomy enough the night before, but today it was even more depressing in comparison with the cheery kitchen.

Irena sat down at the place that had been set for her with Wedgewood china and old polished silver. A crisp linen napkin was folded neatly beside the plate. Hers was the only place set at the table.

Femolly came out of the kitchen carrying the percolator. She poured fragrant chicory coffee into Irena's cup.

"Eggs be ready in a minute."

"Isn't Paul here?" Irena asked.

"Nope."

"I looked into his room. His bed looked as though it hadn't been slept in."

"That so?"

Femolly retreated through the swinging door to the kitchen without further comment. Irena decided that asking direct questions was not the way to get information around here.

The tall woman came back in with a platter of fluffy scrambled eggs and strips of lean bacon. She served a generous portion onto Irena's plate.

"It looks like a pretty day outside," Irena remarked.

"Mm-hmm."

"I was hoping Paul could show me around the city today."

"Shoot, child, you want to see New Orleans, you don't need your brother to drag you around. Every corner got somebody selling a guidebook to the tourists. Down in the Quarter you can't step off the curb without a sightseeing bus running over you. You want to see Uptown, our own St. Charles streetcar as good a way as any."

"I thought Paul might be able to show me some out-of-the-way places."

"Maybe, but if you're willing to spend a few dollars, any taxi driver will take you places even the mayor don't know about. There's hot toast coming."

Femolly barged out through the swinging door again and returned a moment later with a covered plate of toasted sourdough bread and a dish of creamy butter.

"I guess that's what I'll do, then," Irena said, "ride down to the French Quarter and take a sightseeing bus from there."

Femolly's tone softened. "You'll have a good time. People in New Orleans are friendly and always ready to help you out if you got a question."

"Yes, I'm sure I'll find my way around," Irena said. "I'm a little disappointed, that's all."

"Don't let your brother's comin's and goin's bother you, child. His preacher work is a lot like doctorin'. Sometimes he gets a call in the middle of the night and he's got to go rushin' off someplace or other. People call up a doctor to heal the body, and somebody like your brother to heal the soul."

Femolly relaxed into a smile. "Only thing is, you have to look a long time today before you find a doctor who come out in the middle of the night to see you."

"I hope he doesn't have to stay away too long," Irena said. "We haven't really had a chance to talk yet, and there's so much to say."

"You never can tell how long he's gonna be gone," Femolly said. "Sometimes it's two, three days. Other times he's back in a couple hours."

"I suppose I'll just have to make the best of it," Irena said.

"That's the smartest thing to do. You want some more coffee?"

"Not yet, thanks."

"You just holler when you do. I always keep it hot on the stove."

Femolly walked back through the door to the kitchen. Irena admired the woman's regal bearing, her shoulders squared, legs straight and strong under the long skirt. I would like to sketch her, Irena thought.

The idea of sketching cheered her up. She ate the bacon and eggs with more appetite than she believed possible, and drank two more cups of Femolly's coffee.

When she finished breakfast Irena went upstairs and took her sketchbook from the drawer where she had put it. She sharpened half a dozen soft-lead pencils and put them in her tote bag. The sun outside was bright and inviting, the breeze fresh through her window.

She looked into the kitchen to say goodbye to Femolly, then set off to see New Orleans.

Chapter 7

The first stop Irena made was at the Visitor Information Center on Royal Street. There an enthusiastic lady loaded her down with maps, guidebooks, pamphlets, directories and even offered a free cup of New Orleans coffee, which Irena politely declined.

She sat down on a bench to look over the many sightseeing plans available. Finally she chose a fifty-mile bus tour of the entire city, which seemed very reasonable at twelve dollars.

The bus left from the corner of Royal and St. Ann streets. Irena bought a ticket and settled into her seat, aware of a growing sense of depression. Of all the passengers on her bus, happy tourists of all ages, Irena found she was the only one riding alone. There were families, with all their noisy interplay. There were young couples more interested in themselves than the sights of the city. There were middle-aged couples happy to be spending time together without the kids, and older couples who could communicate totally with each other by a touch or a look. Only Irena had no one.

She wondered if ever she would find the special man, the one who was right for her. A man she could do things with, like take this tour of New Orleans. A man she could share with. Share. What a lovely word, even if it was overused these days by pop psychologists. It was a magical word. A process whereby you gave away part of yourself, only to become more of a person than you were before.

The bus started up, and Irena put the lonely thoughts

out of her mind to concentrate on the sights of New Orleans.

They rolled up quiet Esplanade Avenue, then turned down Rampart Street, where old walls had connected the three forts on the northern border of the original city. The driver called their attention to Congo Square, now officially called Beauregard Square, where the slaves were allowed to gather and blow off steam on Saturday nights. They passed the Theatre of the Performing Arts, famous for Mardi Gras balls, and cruised along legendary Basin Street.

The City of the Dead, New Orleans' above-the-ground cemetery, gave Irena a chill. She took more interest in the Quadroon Quarters, where Creole gentlemen had maintained small cottages for their mixed-blood mistresses.

They left the French Quarter then and cruised out Esplanade to the banks of Bayou St. John, then west along the shore of Lake Pontchartrain. On the way back they drove through the Garden District, where Irena marveled at the lovely old homes. These houses, much larger and more lavish than the Gallier house, had been built by the "Uptown" Americans who were determined to outdo the French aristocrats who lived south of Canal Street. The air here was sweet with the floral perfume of the many gardens that gave the district its name.

The last section of New Orleans they saw was the one Irena liked least. Called "Fat City," it provided an alternative to the historic charms of the French Quarter, with modern discotheques, expensive shops, and new restaurants surrounded by steel-and-glass highrise apartment buildings.

When she alighted from the bus back on Royal Street, Irena felt unsatisfied. Everything had gone by too fast. She decided the only way to truly absorb the feeling of the city would be to walk along the narrow old streets and take the time to really look at things. Listen to the special music of New Orleans, inhale the smells, feel its textures. She set out on her own, studying the people, trying to pick up the rhythm of the city.

She came to Jackson Square, at the heart of the French Quarter, and stopped. A dozen artists of varying talent had set up their easels and were brushing on their impressions of the St. Louis Cathedral and the delicately balanced equestrian statue of General Andrew Jackson, his feet firmly planted in the stirrups, hat raised triumphantly aloft.

The sight of the artists at their easels brought back Irena's enthusiasm. She took out her book, found a spot on a stone bench, and began to sketch.

Twenty minutes later Irena snapped the lead of her third pencil in frustration. She could simply not get the cathedral down the way she wanted it. The light was wrong, or she had chosen a poor angle to work from, or she plain wasn't in the mood.

She closed the sketchbook with a snap and walked over to look at the canvases other artists had lined up outside the iron fence with hopefully high price tags attached. There were too many of the familiar weeping clowns and wistful children. The last artist along the fence seemed to be the most talented, although his still lifes were strongly reminiscent of Van Gogh.

"If you like anything, make me an offer," the young artist said from close behind her. "Those prices are just for my ego."

"They're very nice," Irena began, "but I—"

She stopped short, transfixed by one painting that did not seem to belong with the others. It was a white cat, curled up and lying on a dark-blue cushion. There was a spikiness about the fur and a look of madness in the animal's eyes that made Irena shudder.

"It's not very good, is it?" the young artist said.

"It's . . . different."

"The fact is, I don't do animals very well, but some people like them, and I aim to please."

Irena felt suffocated. She had to get away from the terrible painting of the cat.

"Excuse me," she said abruptly to the young artist, and left him standing in front of his paintings as she hurried away. Irena could feel him staring after her.

She walked swiftly up St. Ann Street. The buildings seemed to close in from both sides. The ring of her heels was unnaturally loud in her ears. She stopped, confused, when she found herself at the corner of Bourbon Street.

As always, the sounds of jazz spilled from open doorways as the tourists wandered along both sides of the street. The brassy music and the crowd and the profusion of garish signs made Irena feel dizzy. She looked around for someplace to sit down, and saw she was standing in front of a narrow bar called Le Whiskey. As far as she could tell, it was cool and reasonably empty inside, so she walked in.

The only other customers were a man and a woman in their forties, enthusiastically groping each other in a back booth. Irena found a barstool, and the gray-haired bartender hurried over with a welcoming smile.

"Afternoon, Miss. What can I do for you?"

"I'll have a Coke, please."

"Bourbon and Coke?"

"No, just a Coke."

"Whatever you say." The bartender scooped crushed ice into a glass and filled it with cola from a hose that came up behind the bar.

"Like a twist of lemon in that?"

"No, thank you."

The bartender sighed. He squared up a cocktail

napkin on the bar and placed the glass on it. "I don't feel like I'm doing my job, just pumping Coke into a glass."

Irena smiled at him to show that his efforts were appreciated.

"Quiet today," he said, encouraged by her smile.

"Is it?" Irena had no interest in the state of his business, but it was relaxing to have someone to talk to.

"Yeah, real quiet. It'll pick up about dinnertime, though, then we'll go all night long."

"Sounds exciting."

"Gets to be routine when you've been on the street as many years as I have. Once in a while, though, something really weird happens. Last night, for instance, we had a big ruckus right up in the next block."

"Really?" Irena took a long swallow of the Coke. She was only half-listening to what the man was saying, but the sound of his voice soothed her.

"Oh, yeah, it was something. Had the police, ambulance, fire department. Regular circus."

The man was so plainly eager to talk about it that Irena could not refrain from asking, "What happened?"

"I never did get the whole story, but it seems an escaped lion or something got into a building up the street and got hold of some woman. Chewed her leg right off, is what I hear."

"A lion?" Irena felt a quickening of her interest. The fine hairs quivered at the base of her neck.

"It was some kind of a big cat. Tiger, maybe, I don't know. Whatever it was really kicked up a fuss. Had a big crowd in here after it was over, but no two people seemed to have the same story about what happened."

Irena finished her Coke and set the glass down on the bar with a thump.

"Another one?"

"No, thank you. I have to go." She gathered up her sketchbook and her tote bag and headed out the door.

"Have a nice day," the bartender said, but she was already gone.

Irena walked down Bourbon Street aimlessly for a block. She was troubled by fragments of memory and unformed thoughts that she was afraid to examine too closely. On an impulse she stopped at a pay telephone and looked up the address of the Tabernacle Mission in the book.

The mission turned out to be a barny wooden frame building on North Rampart Street. It was badly in need of painting. Irena climbed the worn wooden steps and pushed open the door. About a dozen men and two or three women were scattered throughout the rows of benches. The odor of their unwashed bodies mingled with the smell of varnish. They were shabby and defeated-looking. Up in front, standing behind a peeling altar, an earnest man with plump cheeks and a rosy complexion was telling the people how to find riches within themselves by declaring for Jesus. The listeners seemed unconvinced.

A young woman with a clean-scrubbed face came up beside Irena.

"Hello, I'm Marianne. Is there something I can help you with?"

"I wonder if Paul Gallier is here. I'm Irena Gallier, his sister."

"No, Paul hasn't been in today. We don't usually see him more than twice a week." Hastily she added, "Not that we aren't grateful for the time he does give us."

"I see." Irena cleared her throat. "Might someone have called him down here last night?"

"Called him down?"

"I mean, might there have been an emergency or something?"

The young woman smiled. "We really don't have that kind of emergency here." She glanced around at the people slouching on the varnished benches. "Mostly all we get is people who are spiritually tired. They're willing to listen to the Word in exchange for a bit of food afterward. As you can see, we don't get much of a crowd. They could do much better by applying for welfare or food stamps, but our people are the kind who don't like the government's getting involved in their lives."

"Then you haven't seen my brother, today or last night?" Irena said.

"Sorry."

Irena thanked the girl and left the mission, slipping a bill into the offering box on her way out. Suddenly she felt very tired. Rather than walk all the way to Carondelet Street to catch the St. Charles trolley home, she hailed a taxi out in front of the mission.

When she got back to the Gallier house, Paul still had not returned. Femolly had prepared a dinner of baked chicken with a flaky crust flavored with herbs. Irena ate without enthusiasm.

"Did my brother call, or anything?" she asked.

"Nope," Femolly said. "Like I told you, sometimes he's gone two, three days. You mustn't worry, he'll come back when he can."

The dark woman disappeared into the kitchen then, and did not return until Irena had finished eating. She started to clear away the dishes, but Irena stopped her with a hand on her arm.

"Femolly, did you know my mother and father?"

"I knew them, child. Worked for them right here in this house, same as I do for your brother and you. They weren't here a whole lot, but I always kept the place ready for when they came."

"What kind of people were they?" Irena asked. "I've

tried and tried, but I can't really remember anything about them."

Femolly's eyes looked into the distance. "They were fine people. Special people. Your father was the handsomest man you'd ever see. He did his best to live the right kind of life. And your mother, your beautiful mother, she looked a lot like you. Oh, they were a fine couple to look at. Truly a handsome couple."

"Did they . . . do you think they loved each other?"

"Oh my, yes. Those were two people as much in love as I ever saw."

"Then why did he . . . I mean, how could he . . . do what he did?"

Femolly looked at her accusingly. "I thought you didn't remember any of that stuff."

"I don't, really, but people have told me about how they died. I went to a library and read the stories that were in the newspaper about it at the time."

"Best you just forget all about it," Femolly said. "Stuff like that is best left buried."

Irena wanted to ask more questions, but Femolly made it clear by the way she clanked the dishes together that the discussion was over.

"You must be tired from walkin' all over town," she said, relenting a little. "Why don't you go on up to bed?"

"I am tired," Irena admitted, "but I don't think I can sleep."

"Why don't you go into the den and look at the television in there? The stuff they got on nowadays always puts me to sleep."

"I think I'll do that," Irena said.

She found the cozy room—all leather and books, with a massive old desk—just off the entrance hall. The air held a faint scent of pipe tobacco. Irena wondered if her father had relaxed in this room. It was not a room that would suit Paul.

She snapped on the small television set and waited for it to warm up. It did not much matter to her what was on, just so it would occupy a part of her mind. When the picture came into focus she settled into a deep, comfortable chair. The story on the screen had something to do with policemen in San Francisco. Irena did not even try to figure out what was going on. The clipped dialog, the multiple gunshots, and the squealing tires during the car chase had a familiar rhythm that relaxed her.

The movie ended and the late news came on. Irena dozed comfortably through the current international crises and the sports report, then snapped suddenly alert as the anchorman switched to local news.

An angry black face filled the screen. Then the camera pulled back to show the leopard sitting against the rear wall of a small cage, glaring out at the camera. The voice of a woman reporter was saying, ". . . the leopard was taken to the New Orleans Zoo, where it is being kept in this quarantine cage while tests are made to determine if it is diseased. So far, attempts to locate the owner have been unsuccessful."

The camera pulled back still farther to include in the picture a slim, windblown young woman standing next to the cage and talking into a ball-on-a-stick microphone.

"If no owner turns up," the reporter said, "the zoo will have to decide what to do with its new kitty cat. This is Christine Goode at the New Orleans Zoo."

Irena sat in the chair staring at the screen during the remainder of the news and a rerun of *Starsky and Hutch* without seeing any of it. Sometime after midnight she went to bed and slept fitfully, her dreams filled with cats.

Chapter 8

In the morning Irena awoke with a light sheen of perspiration covering her body. The bedroom curtains hung limp before the open window. Outside the sky was low and gray over the city, holding the heat and moisture in like a lid on a pot.

Irena got out of bed and walked down the hall to Paul's room. Again there was no answer to her knock. Inside everything was exactly as it had been the day before. The bed was neatly made, the window open, everything precisely in its place.

She dressed and went down to breakfast, but asked no questions this morning about her brother's whereabouts. Nor did Femolly offer any information. The breakfast of buttermilk pancakes was served and eaten in silence.

"Is there a newspaper?" Irena asked as the dark woman cleared away the dishes.

Femolly shook her head. "Your brother don't hold with newspapers. Can't say as I blame him. Nothing but killings and wars and other bad news."

Irena went into the den and turned on the television set. She clicked from channel to channel, looking for a newscast, but found nothing but game shows and reruns of ancient situation-comedies. Frustrated, she snapped off the set and went back up to her room.

For an hour she poked around, arranging and rearranging the things in her drawers and the wardrobe chest. She critically studied the sketch she had begun yesterday of the St. Louis Cathedral. It still did not look right. She tore the page from the spiral-bound book, crumpled it into a ball, and dropped it into the wastebasket.

Growing more restless by the minute, she stepped through the window onto the balcony that stretched across the front of the house. She leaned on the iron railing for a while and watched the cars that moved up and down the street under the heavy old elm trees.

Finally it became impossible to stay in the house. Irena gathered up her sketchbook and tote bag and went downstairs. She found Femolly in the kitchen, sitting at the red-checkered table, doing a crossword puzzle.

"I'm going out for a while," Irena said.

Femolly's answer was a noncommittal grunt.

"Do you think I'll need a raincoat? The clouds look kind of threatening."

"Won't rain today," Femolly said, looking up briefly.

Irena hesitated for a moment. "Well, I'll see you later." She left the house with Femolly's eyes following her.

The St. Charles streetcar took her downtown, where she found a taxi and told the driver where she wanted to go.

After a few minutes the taxi rolled to a stop before a tall gate in a red brick wall. A dilapidated ticket booth stood outside the gate. Beyond the bars a few gloomy buildings of Southern Gothic architecture were visible. People strolled the grounds unhurriedly.

"Is this it?" Irena asked the driver.

"This is what you asked for, lady. The old New Orleans Zoo."

Irena fished in her bag for money to pay the fare.

"Sure you wouldn't rather see the French Quarter?" the driver said.

"I've seen the French Quarter."

"If it's a zoo you want, why not let me take you to Audubon Park? It's bigger, newer, cleaner, and there's a lot more to do there."

"No, thank you," Irena said. "This is the one I want."

The driver shrugged, took her money, and drove off, shaking his head over some tourists' peculiar ideas of fun.

Irena paid a dollar at the ticket booth and walked through the rusting iron gate into the old zoo. It did not have the open, antiseptic look of more modern establishments, but there was a certain scruffy charm to the place.

The air was cooler in the zoo than out in the city, thanks to the profusion of trees and shrubbery. Irena inhaled deeply, enjoying the raw, wild scent of the animals.

The tourists who wandered about the old zoo were a different breed than the hurrying, anxious crowds that milled up and down Bourbon Street. For the most part they were older, more conservatively dressed, and seemingly under no compulsion to see everything in one day. And there were children here. One group of dark-eyed youngsters was shepherded along by a pair of nuns dressed in the old traditional habit. The children chattered happily in Spanish while the nuns clucked over them.

As Irena strolled past a gift shop near the entrance, an elderly man and woman came out wearing new sun visors that had nicknames stitched on the band. *Deedee* and *Big Sam*. They smiled warmly at Irena. She smiled back, then continued down the path following a sign that read: *Primates*.

She passed a large cage where twenty or so South American monkeys clambered about the concrete ledges and swung through the branches of a dead tree. Their bright little eyes watched the people walking by. Irena

78

did not linger. She had never liked monkeys. Their behavior was too much like that of humans. It embarrassed her. If you stood long enough before a cage full of monkeys you would recognize most of the human foibles. There were the bullies and the cowards, the sneaks and the show-offs. And always there was a forlorn loner, smaller than the rest, that the others picked on. Too much like humans.

Irena walked on until the sound of a voice brought her to a stop in front of a cage containing two orangutans. The voice was coming from a small speaker box in front of the cage, into which a family of tourists had inserted a dime. Irena edged closer to listen.

". . . Fewer than three thousand of these playful, intelligent creatures are left in the world today, thanks to the depredations of Man, who continues to destroy their natural habitat."

The voice was that of a young man. The tone had a warmth and sincerity to it that appealed to Irena. She could believe that the speaker truly cared about the animals.

". . . The pair you are looking at now, Dante and Josie, were born in captivity. They are products of artificial insemination. This is usually the case today, as civilization does not seem to stir up romantic feelings in the orangutan."

The two adults in the tourist family tittered at this. Irena smiled.

". . . The zoo today is like a modern ark. We are fighting to guarantee the survival of the earth's endangered species, and serving when we can as a breeding ground to ensure that our animals will not vanish."

The speaker clicked off and the two orangutans applauded, bringing a laugh from the tourists. Irena continued along the path.

A pair of mandrills, with doglike faces and bright

79

blue rumps, watched her with interest. She passed them without stopping. Also a pair of bored-looking chimpanzees.

At the end of the primate section was the glassed-in reptile house. Irena walked in and joined a group in front of one of the cases to see what the attraction was. Inside a python, twelve feet long and thick as a man's arm, glided toward a white rat that was sitting hunched and paralyzed with fear. As the snake unhinged its jaws, many of the people watching turned away, shuddering. Irena continued to watch, fascinated, as the python took the rat whole into its mouth and began the undulating process of swallowing it live.

When Irena left the reptile house she stood indecisively for a moment where the path branched off in two directions. Off to her left she could see the bear cages. The heavy animals stood on their hind feet and clowned and waved at the people, begging for peanuts. Bears were the big crowd-pleasers of any zoo.

Irena looked down the branch of the path that went to the right. A few yards along, a sign in the shape of an arrow read: *Big Cats.* And she knew this was why she had come. Ever since she had seen the black leopard on the television news last night, Irena had been drawn here. She could not say exactly why she had to come, but she knew it would have been impossible to stay away.

With no more hesitation she walked down the path toward the cats. The lions were the first she came to. Great shaggy-maned beasts with wide-set amber eyes and placid expressions that revealed nothing of what they were thinking. Irena stopped in front of the cage to admire them. One old male sat on a rock ledge, well above the others. The patriarch. On the floor of the cage a younger male prowled restlessly from one side of the cage to the other and back again. In the jungle he would be nearing the time when he would challenge the older lion for leadership. Four females dozed beside a shallow concrete pool. A pair of cubs batted energetically at each other under the watchful eye of their mother.

Irena moved along to the cage where the tigers were. There were two of them, a male and a female. They padded ceaselessly back and forth, back and forth, moving with a sensual grace. They stopped their pacing when Irena drew near, and turned to look at her.

Irena moved close to the cage. An excitement that was close to sexual welled up inside her. The tigers were both beautiful and frightening, like gods in orange and black. The muscles moved smoothly in their mighty shoulders and haunches.

"Hello," she said softly through the bars. "Hello, my beautiful friends."

The tigers stood motionless a few feet away, watching, waiting.

It seemed to Irena that her senses were more keenly alert than at any time in her life. A powerful feeling of belonging overcame her. It was a feeling she had never known.

Finally she turned away from the tigers and continued along the path. She had not gone far when she spied a small gap in the brush along one side. She investigated and found a narrow trail, faint and partially overgrown, that led away at right angles from the main path. A new scent reached her nostrils, and Irena knew that this was the way she must go.

A short way down the new trail her way was barred by a chain stretched across between two metal posts. A sign hanging from the chain read:

No Admittance
Animal In Quarantine

Without pausing, Irena raised the chain and ducked under it. She followed the narrow trail through a patch of trees. Up ahead she could hear voices. A man was cursing violently. A woman seemed to be trying to calm him. An undertone to the argument was the soft growling of a big cat.

Irena pushed back a last clump of brush and saw the cage about thirty feet away. Beyond it the path led into a small wooded area, then up a grassy slope on the far side to an old brick building. As Irena watched, the man, who was dressed in jeans and a T-shirt, headed into the trees. He walked with a stiff and unnatural gait. The woman remained behind, hosing down the floor of the cage. She was careful to direct the stream of water away from the animal inside.

Finally the woman picked up something she had in a plastic bag and followed the man. Irena waited until she saw first the man, then the woman, climb the grassy bank and enter the building. Then she left the concealment of the brush and approached the cage.

Chapter 9

On the far side of the quarantine cage, beyond a dense patch of trees and atop a grassy bank, sat the aged administration building of the New Orleans Zoo. Inside, in a ground-floor laboratory, Oliver Yates was using surgical forceps to assist a poisonous snake in shedding its skin. Oliver plucked gently at the drying husk, taking care not to injure the shiny new skin beneath it.

"Amazing process, isn't it?" he said to the other man in the room. "When they outgrow an old skin they just slough it off, and there's a brand-new one underneath. Sort of like being reborn. It's too bad we humans can't do something like that when our skins outlive their usefulness."

Bronte Judson perched on a stool and carefully kept his eyes averted from what Oliver was doing with the snake. Despite the heat, he wore a three-piece suit, with a necktie severely knotted at the collar of his white shirt. To Judson's way of thinking, the title of Chief Administrator required him to maintain a certain formality.

"Never mind the snake," Judson said. "We've got to make a decision soon about what to do with the black leopard."

"What's to decide?" Oliver said, without looking up from the shedding snake. "Once he's out of quarantine, providing nobody claims him, we free up one of our other exhibits, give him some space to move around, and we've got ourselves a new attraction that didn't cost us a dime."

"Isn't it possible that he's dangerous?"

Oliver put down the forceps and turned to face the administrator. "Dangerous? Hell, yes, he's dangerous. They're all dangerous. What do you think we're running here, a puppy farm?"

"I know, I know," Judson said, "but this one seems ... different. I had a look at him this morning, and I tell you that animal scared me, even with the steel bars between us. He doesn't act like the other cats."

"There *is* something about him," Oliver admitted. "His behavior doesn't fit the normal patterns. That's one reason I wired Dr. Fritch in San Francisco to come down and have a look at him."

"San Francisco?" Judson's voice cracked.

"That's right. Fritch is the best big-cat man in the country."

"But San Francisco! What's that going to cost us?"

"Who knows?" Oliver said. "That's your department. You're the money man, I'm the animal man."

"Damn it, Oliver, you know the trouble we've been having getting any funds out of the city. They want to close this place down and give all the money to Audubon. How am I supposed to justify the expense of bringing a cat doctor all the way out here from California?"

"Don't tell them what it's for. Juggle the accounts around to absorb the expense somewhere else."

Judson shook his head sadly. "Oliver, Oliver, you just don't understand the fiscal problems in running a zoo today. Or the politics involved either, for that matter."

"I understand this much—flying Fritch out here will cost us a whole lot less than buying our own leopard would."

"Who says we need a leopard? We've done just fine without a black leopard so far. Why do we want one now?"

"Because he's here, Bronte," Oliver said patiently.

"Whether we want a black leopard or not, we've got one, and it's our responsibility to take care of him. Have you any other suggestions?"

Judson seemed to look at something off in a corner. We could euthanize it."

"Kill him? Are you serious?"

Judson forced his gaze back up to meet Oliver's. "It might be the best solution all around."

"Tell me how it's best for the leopard."

The administrator pursed his lips. "I think you're getting a Dr. Doolittle complex. Let me remind you that this is a zoo, not a shelter for homeless animals. The city expects us to turn a profit here, however small, and your salary and mine depend on that. The animals are, in a sense, our product. They are not our family."

"I will not consider euthanasia of the leopard," Oliver said adamantly.

"Can't we at least discuss it?"

"No, we cannot. These animals are not television sets or boxes of oatmeal. They are living, breathing creatures." Oliver's voice rose as he warmed to his subject. "We brought them here, we have a responsibility to them. It's because of men that they aren't living free in their natural surroundings. Men destroy their environment, then bring them here and put them in cages for other men to look at. It's up to people like you and me to make it as comfortable for these captive creatures as we possibly can. If one of them doesn't act just exactly the way we think he should, we don't shoot him full of poison, we try to find out what's bothering him, and help him."

"Oliver, I—" Judson began.

Oliver ignored him and plowed on. "What the hell do you think I do this for? The money? I've got offers from four universities in this country and one in Mexico

City. Any one of them would start me out at twice what I'm making here. I'll tell you why I stay at this relic of a zoo, I stay because the animals here need somebody who cares about them. *I* care about them. That's my job."

Bronte Judson held up his hands in surrender. "All right, Oliver, enough. You've made your point. Go ahead and bring out this California doctor for your leopard. I'll see what I can do about squeezing a few more dollars out of the city fathers. After all, that's *my* job."

Oliver relaxed slowly and grinned at the administrator. "Bronte, underneath that skinflint exterior, I believe you might have a heart after all."

"Don't count on it," Judson said. "I just know when I've been out-talked."

The door to the laboratory burst open, startling both men, and Joe Creigh stumbled in. His face was a mask of disgust. He held his hands awkwardly away from his body. The T-shirt and jeans he wore were covered with a thick fluid full of pulpy lumps. A sickly, sour odor came into the lab with him.

"What happened to you?" Oliver said.

"The sonofabitch puked on me."

"The leopard?"

"Who the hell do you think?"

"What were you doing in the cage?"

"He looked half asleep. I was just trying to get a vitamin pill down him and the sonofabitch puked all over me."

"I told you to let me handle the medication on that cat," Oliver said.

"Believe me, you can handle it from now on," Joe said with feeling. "Black sonofabitch puked on me."

Bronte Judson edged over next to an open window.

"Do you suppose he could go somewhere and change those clothes?"

"Go on down to the locker room and shower," Oliver told the young man. "You'll find a pair of coveralls down there you can put on."

"The sonofabitch—"

"I know," Oliver cut him off, "he puked on you."

Joe slouched out of the room.

Oliver turned to Bronte Judson. "I always said animals can act very human sometimes."

The door opened again and Alice Moore came in. She carried a sealed plastic bag.

"Hi." Alice sniffed at the air. "I see Joe has already been here."

"He just left. Where were you when the sonofabitch puked on him?"

"I was collecting a stool sample. I don't know what possessed the damn fool to play doctor."

"I don't think he'll do it again."

"Not likely."

Oliver pointed to the plastic bag. "What have you got there?"

"Something rather interesting." She held the bag up so the light from the window revealed its contents. "What would you say it looks like?"

Oliver and Judson moved closer to examine the bag. Oliver looked at the administrator and raised his eyebrows in a question.

Judson said, "It looks like a half-eaten slice of pizza."

Alice smiled at him brightly. "Right the first time, Mr. Judson."

"This is probably a silly question," Oliver said, "but why are you carrying it around with you in a plastic bag?"

"It came up out of the leopard."

Bronte Judson backed away hastily.

"No kidding?" Oliver took the bag from Alice and hefted it. "We have a pizza-eating black leopard. Most unusual species."

"Could somebody have fed it to him this morning?"

"No," Oliver said flatly. "Nobody but you, me, and Joe have been near the quarantine cage."

"Then where did he get it?"

"Probably scrounged it out of a garbage can while he was prowling through the city on his way to the massage parlor."

"Have you figured out what he was doing there?" Alice asked. "From the contents of his stomach, he sure wasn't hungry."

"Maybe he was horny," Oliver said with a leer.

"A most unusual cat," Alice said.

"Are any of the test results in?"

"So far they're all negative. No ascariasis, no distemper, no encephalitis. Except for his erratic behavior and his odd eating habits, this seems to be one healthy cat."

"I've asked Dr. Fritch to fly out from the Coast and take a look at him."

"That's wonderful," Alice said.

"Oh yes, wonderful," Bronte Judson said, with a completely different emphasis.

"The chief administrator is not sold on our new cat," Oliver explained to Alice. "But I'll bet you learn to love him, Bronte."

"I sincerely doubt that." Judson started toward the door. "I'd better go start practicing if I'm going to convince the city fathers that we need a specialist from California to come out and hold your new cat's paw and find out what's making him neurotic."

"You can do it, Bronte," Oliver said as the administrator went out the door.

When they were alone Alice came over and stood

close to Oliver. "It's almost closing time. Got any plans for this evening?"

"I'm going to be working late tonight," he said. "I want to go over all the leopard test results in detail and see if we've missed anything."

"Want me to stay and help?"

"Thanks, but there really isn't much for you to do."

"Will you call me if you finish up early?"

"I promise."

"All right, then. See you."

When Alice had gone Oliver picked up the plastic bag and held it to the light.

"Pizza," he said to the empty laboratory. "That's strange. Very strange."

Chapter 10

The cage was some twelve feet square. There were heavy bars on three of the walls. The fourth was solid metal. A wooden shelf, six feet long by three feet deep, was fastened halfway up the back wall. The cage looked for all the world like a prison cell.

At the rear of the cage, half hidden in the shadows, sat the black leopard. For what seemed to her like an eternity, Irena and the cat had been regarding each other silently.

"You poor creature," Irena said at last. "Oh, I'm so sorry." The cat was in distress. It gave no outward signs, but somehow Irena knew. She *knew*.

"Are you in pain?" she asked softly.

The cat did not move.

"No, it's a hurt deeper than that, isn't it," Irena continued. "You're a prisoner here. Locked up. They have taken your freedom. There is nothing worse than that. I understand."

The leopard cocked his head, watching her with unblinking yellow eyes.

"You are such a magnificent thing," Irena said. "What a shame it is to keep you locked up like this. I wonder where your home is. I mean your real home. I'll bet you miss it."

She took a tentative step toward the cage. The leopard stood up. Its muscles tensed under the shiny black coat. Irena stopped.

"I'm not going to hurt you. I would never do anything to hurt you. You know that, don't you?"

The cat blinked its eyes.

"You do trust me, don't you? Has someone here been mistreating you?"

Moving in graceful slow motion, the leopard approached the bars at the front of the cage where Irena stood.

"It's all right," she crooned. "You can come closer to me. I'm your friend."

The big cat reached the bars, his eyes never leaving Irena's face. A red rasp of a tongue slid out and ran over the shiny black leather of his nose.

"Yes, you are a lovely thing," Irena told the cat in a soothing voice. "I wonder if you know how beautiful you are."

She sat down on the spongy grass a few feet away from the cage. She opened her sketchbook and placed it on her lap. From the tote bag she took a freshly sharpened soft-lead pencil.

"I'm going to draw your picture," she said. "Would you like that? You and I will just sit here and talk, and I'll draw your picture."

The leopard rotated his sleek head and growled from deep in his throat. There was no threat in the growl. It was more like a greeting.

Irena smiled in answer. "You're glad I've come, aren't you? I can tell. I can almost tell what you're thinking. Almost."

The leopard sat, straight and proud, as though he were posing for her. Irena poised the pencil over her sketchbook and began to draw.

As she filled page after page with studies of the leopard she lost all sense of time and place. She was completely unaware of the gradual darkening of the sky and the exodus of the people from the main zoo. Here in this sheltered nook nothing existed, except the big cat and herself.

*   *   *

Up in the administration building Oliver Yates sat hunched over his cluttered desk. The sky grew dark outside the window, but he paid no attention. Over and over he read the reports prepared by the city veterinarians who had examined the black leopard. Nothing in the reports indicated that there was anything physically wrong with the cat. And yet, something definitely *was* wrong.

For one thing, there was the sheer size of the creature. A mature young male, it weighed in at 240 pounds, almost 100 pounds more than the average for the species. The cat's measurements—height, girth, length, paw print—all far exceeded the norm. Oliver could find no explanation for any of this in the medical reports. All he could do was hope that Dr. Fritch could shed some light on the situation when he arrived from the Coast.

Even more puzzling than the size of the cat was the mystery of where it came from. Naturally the two black leopards housed across the city at the big Audubon Park Zoo had been checked out at once, and had been found snug and secure in the cages where they belonged. A query to all circuses that might conceivably have been in the area also came up negative.

The idea that some private citizen in New Orleans had been keeping a black leopard in his back yard was preposterous. Yet there seemed to be no other explanation. Every known cat within a five-hundred-mile radius of the city had been accounted for.

The whole affair became more puzzling, the deeper Oliver dug into it. Even assuming that someone in the city were foolish enough to keep an illegal carnivorous wild animal as a pet, and further assuming that he was now too frightened to come forward and claim it, how the devil could a 240-pound black leopard make his way along Bourbon Street, one of the busiest streets in the world, and stroll up a flight of stairs to a massage parlor without being seen by even one person? It was a question that Sergeant Brant and the whole New Orleans Police Department had not been able to answer, and it sure as hell baffled Oliver Yates.

The young curator pushed his chair back from the desk and pinched his eyes together. He had not slept much since the big cat came into his life. Hadn't even relaxed much. Maybe, he thought, he should have let Alice stay tonight, as she had offered. She would have been pleasant company. And now they could leave together, go to his place for a tension-easing drink or two, and go to bed.

Oliver was genuinely fond of Alice. He admired her as a professional in the same line of work. And her physical attributes did not escape him either. He enjoyed their dates together and their lovemaking. But he was not in love with her.

Lately he had begun to worry that Alice's feelings for him were going beyond the limits of good fun. It could make for an uncomfortable working situation. No, he decided, it was best that he sent her on home tonight. In fact, he resolved to start gradually cooling the whole relationship.

His musings along this line were interrupted by a roar from the direction of the quarantine cage. It was not a cry of pain or distress, but somehow carried a feeling of joy.

Oliver raised his head to listen. The cat roared again.

Oliver swiveled his chair to face the window. "What's going on with you, big fella?" It was a good excuse to leave the desk work and go down to have a look.

He left the building and made his way down the slope toward the little grove of trees. Beyond them the leopard's cage was in deep shadow. Oliver fancied he could hear sounds coming from the vicinity of the quarantine cage, but he could not be sure. The night creatures of the zoo were talking to one another.

He pushed his way through the brush at the bottom of the slope and into the trees, muttering at himself for not bringing a flashlight. He made slow progress, as tree branches smacked him in the face and roots seemed to reach out and clutch at his ankles.

When at last he came out at the far side of the clump of trees he stopped. The clouds that had hung over the city all day parted, and the scene was bathed in chilly moonlight.

Oliver's heart jumped. A shout caught in his throat at what he saw. The moon was bright enough now that there could be no doubt. Someone was standing at the leopard's cage. Standing right up against the bars. And although he could not be sure at this distance, it looked for all the world as though the night visitor was reaching right into the cage.

He choked back the impulse to cry out a warning. Moving as swiftly and silently as he could, Oliver crossed the grassy patch between the trees and the cage. If he made any noise that startled the person or the leopard now, tragedy could be the result.

There had been instances of teenagers mindlessly mauling the animals—shooting the deer with a .22 rifle, slitting the throats of harmless mountain goats. Many times Oliver had thought if he could get his hands on one of those cretinous children he would happily cripple him.

However, as he drew closer to the quarantine cage he saw that this was no attack on his animal. The black leopard, like an overgrown kitty cat, was rubbing his head against the bars, clearly enjoying the attention he was getting. And he could now see that the figure on the outside of the bars was, surprisingly, a woman.

Stealthily, Oliver moved up behind her. He could hear her talking to the cat.

"That feels good, does it? I thought it would. I have always liked to have the back of my neck rubbed. Poor darling, to be so cruelly held captive here. If I could open the door for you and let you run free, I would. Do you know that? Yes, you do know, don't you? We have a feeling for each other, you and I. A special feeling. A closeness that many people never have."

For a moment Oliver had the giddy feeling that he was interrupting a pair of lovers. He shook it off and crept up quietly behind the girl. Under his breath he prayed that no twig would snap beneath his foot and turn the bizarre tableau into a bloody nightmare. The leopard, he could see, had his head down as the girl dug her fingers into the short, thick fur behind his ears. Sensuously she massaged the corded neck muscles.

When he was as close as he dared go, Oliver leaped at the girl. He caught her around the waist and fell backward, pulling her down on top of him. He hit the ground hard, and for several seconds just lay there on his back, maintaining his hold on the girl. He felt the wild beating of her heart. He also felt the slim supple waist and the soft undercurve of the girl's breasts. Embarrassingly, he began to get an erection.

The girl pulled in a lungful of air, and Oliver was afraid she was going to scream.

"Please be calm," he said, making his own voice as casual as possible. "I'm the curator here. My name is Oliver Yates. I'm not going to hurt you."

For a moment the only sound was their breathing. The leopard growled and hit the bars a clanging blow with one paw.

"Do you have to hold me so tightly?" the girl asked.

"Sorry."

Oliver eased his grip on the girl. Then, when he felt

she was not going to bolt, he released her. They both stood up, brushing bits of grass and dirt from their clothing. For a man who had just saved a girl's life, Oliver felt strangely embarrassed.

"Just what did you think you were doing here?" he asked.

"I was sketching the leopard."

"Sketching, you say?"

"That's right." The girl looked around on the grass until she spied a spiral-bound book. She picked it up and held it for Oliver to see while she flipped the pages. He could not see clearly what was on the pages in the moonlight, but it seemed to be drawings of the leopard, as the girl had said. There were head studies, upper body, and full length. Oliver started to examine the drawings critically, then realized the absurdity of the situation.

"Sketching, hell," he said angrily. "You had your hand inside the cage."

"That was after I was all through drawing. I was petting him."

"Petting him? I can't believe I'm hearing this. Did you say you were petting my leopard?"

"Of course. Couldn't you see that? He was upset when I got here. Something happened earlier that disturbed him. And he was very lonely. I don't believe anyone here has shown him any love."

Oliver stared at her. "You're serious, aren't you?"

"Yes, of course I'm serious."

"Don't you realize that this is a highly dangerous animal? We know for a fact that he's mauled one woman severely. God only knows what other mayhem he's responsible for."

"Pooh. All he needs is some affection."

"Oh, you could sense that, could you?"

"As a matter of fact, I could," she said, ignoring the

sarcasm. "And if you're supposed to be the . . . what did you call yourself?"

"Curator."

"If you're the curator here, I should think you could sense things about animals too."

"I can, sometimes," Oliver said in a gentler tone. "But I still wouldn't go poking my arm into the cage of an animal who could rip it off with a swipe of his paw."

"I was in no danger," she said.

In the moonlight Oliver saw that the girl had a nice smile. An exceptionally nice smile.

"You know who I am now," he said; "how about making us even?"

"I'm Irena Gallier."

"Welcome to the New Orleans Zoo, Miss Gallier. It is *miss?*"

"It is."

"I'll be glad to show you around personally next time, but it might be better if you come during the hours when we're open to the public."

"I'm sorry," she said. "I guess I lost track of the time."

Her knees seemed to weaken suddenly. She staggered, and Oliver reached out to catch her.

"Are you all right?"

"I—I think so. Just a little dizzy for a moment."

She was light and vulnerable-feeling in his arms. Oliver put a hand to her forehead. He found it hot and dry to his touch.

"You're feverish," he said.

She leaned against him. "Your hand feels so nice and cool."

"Can you walk all right?"

"Oh, yes, if I can lean on you a little."

"My pleasure. Come on, and I'll take you up to the ad building. There's a dispensary there."

"No, really, I think I'll be all right in a minute," she said.

"I'll be the judge of that. Did I tell you that I'm a doctor?"

"No, you didn't. A medical doctor?"

He smiled down at her. "Not exactly, but I can at least get you an aspirin."

"You're the doctor," she said weakly.

Behind them, the leopard growled softly as they started away.

Irena let herself be led through the trees and up the grassy slope to the administration building. Oliver took her into the small dispensary and persuaded her to lie down on the couch. He soaked a cloth under cold running water, wrung it out, and laid it gently across her forehead.

"No kidding," she said, "I don't want to be any trouble to you."

"Hush. If I can find a thermometer, I'll take your temperature and we'll see if we ought to call a genuine doctor for you."

He took a bottle of pills from a shelf, shook two into his hand, and gave them to her with a plastic cup of water.

"In the meantime, take these."

"I don't much believe in medicine."

"It's only aspirin."

"I don't need it. Really, I feel all right now."

Irena took the damp cloth from her forehead and sat up. She smiled at him.

"See? Good as new."

Oliver looked at her suspiciously. "You sure didn't seem all right a few minutes ago." He came over and put his hand on her forehead again. Her skin was smooth and cool under his fingers. "That's funny. You were burning up when I brought you in here. Now you feel normal to me."

"I have a peculiar metabolism," she said. "Doctors have told me I don't have the same kind of reactions that other people do."

"A medical marvel," he said.

"In a way. I don't like doctors. I'm glad you're not a real one."

"But I *am* a real one," he told her, a little defensively. "I just happen to be a doctor of zoology instead of medicine."

"Well, that's all right, I suppose."

"Thanks."

"You're not mad at me?"

"No," he said, chuckling, "but somebody ought to be, for the chances you take. Can I get you anything?"

"Well ..." She looked around the dispensary. "I don't suppose there's anything to eat around here. Suddenly I'm starving."

"Not unless you'd like a nice mash of meal worms and crickets."

She made a face.

"Or horsemeat tartare?"

"Yuck."

"I'll tell you what, I'm about to close up shop for the night, and I'm kind of hungry myself. Why don't you come with me?"

"I'd like that," she said.

Oliver blinked in surprise. He had expected her to be coy about it while they went through the usual thrust and parry of making a first date. She really *did* react differently.

"Good," he said. "There's a little steak house not far from here where I stop sometimes."

"I try to stay away from meat," she said.

"Right." He appraised her for a moment, wondering

99

if she was going to turn out to be one of those health food freaks. A displaced flower child—natural child-birth, save the whales, no nukes, and all that.

"What about seafood?" he ventured.

"I love it."

"Wonderful." He breathed an inner sigh of relief. "There are almost as many fish houses in New Orleans as Dixieland bands. Let's go."

When they left the zoo, Oliver saw to it that they did not walk past the black leopard.

Chapter 11

The Little Napoleon Fish House on Toulouse Street was not advertised in the tourist guides. Little attention was paid to atmosphere. However, it was well known to the local people who appreciated good food at a reasonable price and did not need frills.

The Little Napoleon had an oyster bar where a cheerful black man cracked open the shells with hands that moved faster than the eye could follow. The lights were kept low so the plain wooden tables didn't look too shabby. There was no live music and no jukebox, but the door was always open so the customers could enjoy the sounds of a jazz band playing a couple of doors away at the corner of Bourbon Street.

Oliver and Irena sat across from each other at one of the small tables. He watched with a smile as she dipped the last of her half dozen oysters into the spicy sauce and popped it into her mouth.

"Am I doing it wrong?" she said.

"What's that?"

"The way you were looking at me, I thought maybe I was eating the oysters wrong."

Oliver laughed. "Not that I'm aware of. I'm just glad to see that you have such a hearty appetite. For a while, back there, I was afraid that you were a really sick girl."

"I told you I have a strange metabolism."

"Maybe so, but there's sure nothing wrong with the rest of you."

"Are you flirting with me, Mr. Curator?" she said.

"Just a little. Laying the groundwork, you might say."

Irena studied his face. "You don't look much like a curator."

"Oh? What does a curator look like?"

"Older, for one thing. Gray hair, getting thin on top. Wire-rim glasses. A slight stoop. Jacket with leather patches at the elbows."

"I do have one of those jackets at home."

"You still don't fit the image."

"If not a curator, what *do* I look like?"

Irena put two fingers to her cheek thoughtfully. "I don't know. Maybe a high-school football coach. Or somebody who races cars. Or a mountain climber."

"Those all sound very glamorous," he said, "but what I am is the curator of the New Orleans Zoo."

The waiter arrived with two platters of flaky pompano caught that morning in Breton Sound. It was served with lemon-butter sauce and feather-light French fries.

"They have a pretty good house chablis here," Oliver said.

"If you don't mind, I'd rather have a glass of milk."

"Why should I mind?" To the waiter he said, "One glass of milk and a small carafe of chablis."

"I'm not much of a drinker," she apologized.

"That *is* a shame, because I was planning to get you drunk and have my way with you."

"Oho, so that's why you were feeding me all those oysters."

"It was worth a try," he said with an elaborate shrug.

Irena took a bite of the pompano and closed her eyes in pleasure. "This is delicious. I *do* love fish."

Oliver smiled, sharing her enjoyment.

The waiter brought the milk and the wine. Irena and Oliver toasted each other.

"So are you going to tell me just what the curator of a zoo does?" she said.

"Are you really interested?"

"Of course I am. I wouldn't have asked you otherwise."

"I'm not a vet myself, but I oversee the veterinary work. Do a lot of research. I'm responsible for buying the animals, when we have the budget for it. I also sell animals when we have a surplus of a particular breed. Set up the exhibits. And sometimes, when we get a donation or win a government grant, I'll head up an expedition."

"An expedition? Like into the jungle?"

"Sometimes."

"Now, that sounds exciting. You see, I knew there was something glamorous about you."

"I'm glad you think so, but most of my expeditions are into the bureaucratic jungles. A lot of the local politicians don't think New Orleans needs two zoos. Between you and me, they just may be right."

"How long have you done this kind of work?"

"Ever since I got out of college. That would be almost ten years now. But it really started when I was a kid. I was always comfortable around animals. Spent more time with them than I did with people. I still do, if you come right down to it."

"I love animals too," Irena said seriously. "They're so, I don't know, honest."

"I know what you mean." Oliver grinned suddenly. "I never knew a monkey who would cheat on his golf score."

Irena smiled politely.

"But that's enough of the Oliver Yates story for one evening. Tell me about yourself. Where do you come from? What are you doing in New Orleans? How did I happen to find you with your hand in my leopard's mouth?"

"Which question do you want me to answer first?" she said.

"Take your choice."

"What am I doing in New Orleans? I'm looking for a job. I thought my brother, Paul, was going to help me, but he's been busy and I haven't even seen him since I got in two days ago. I'm just marking time until I get a chance to talk to him."

"What kind of a job are you looking for?"

"Eventually I want to get into commercial art. That's what I studied for. In the meantime I'll take anything I can find to tide me over. I'm good with children. I used to take care of my foster parents' kids a lot."

"Foster parents?"

Irena looked uncomfortable. "Yes. I . . . never knew my real parents."

"Look, it's none of my business. I didn't mean to pry."

"It's all right," she told him, "I don't mind talking about it. A therapist I went to told me it would be good for me to talk about it." She drew a deep breath and continued. "When I was four years old my father shot my mother to death, then killed himself. Some kind of a love triangle."

Oliver reached across the table and took her hand. "You poor kid. I'm so sorry."

"It was a long time ago. Seventeen years. Actually, I don't remember anything about it. They tell me I blanked it all out of my mind. A lucky thing, I guess. Still, sometimes I wonder about them, my mother and father. What they were like. In the pictures I've seen, they made a very good-looking couple."

"I'm not surprised," Oliver said. "They have good-looking children."

"My brother will be pleased to hear that," she said mischievously.

"Uh, look," Oliver began awkwardly, "until you find

something you really want to do, how would you like to work at the zoo?"

Irena's face lit up. "I'd love it! To work around animals all day, I'd almost do it for nothing. But I really don't have any qualifications for that kind of work."

"For what I have in mind," Oliver said, "you wouldn't need any qualifications other than a good personality and a nice smile. And you certainly have those."

" 'Thank you sir,' the maiden said."

"And it's not exactly working with animals, it's in the gift shop. One of the girls there quit suddenly, and we need somebody to fill in until we find a permanent replacement."

"It sounds marvelous. Can you really arrange it?"

"I am not without influence, my dear."

Irena laughed along with him. "I'll bet you're not."

Oliver signaled the waiter to bring the check. He watched as she drank the last of her milk. It left a pale moustache on her upper lip. She licked it off with her pointed pink tongue.

Oliver paid the check and they walked out into the parking lot, where Oliver had left the truck. He helped her in on the passenger side, then went around and got in behind the wheel.

He said, "I don't suppose you'd be interested in coming to my place for a nightcap?"

"On our very first date? I'm afraid you overestimate the power of those oysters."

"I take it that means no."

She smiled and touched his arm. "Not this time, Oliver. I really am very tired."

"Then there will be another time?"

"If you want there to be."

"You can bet on it." Oliver keyed the engine to life. "Where to?"

She gave him the address and they talked easily about inconsequential things as he drove out quiet St. Charles Street. Irena was animated and cheerful. Oliver thought she was incredibly beautiful in the intermittent light from the overhead street lamps.

"That's it," she said, "the house up ahead with no lights."

Oliver pulled to a stop and looked up at the front of the dark brick house behind the forbidding iron fence.

"This is where you live?"

"My brother does. I'm staying here until I can find a place of my own."

"It looks kind of grim."

"Maybe the house reflects the lives of the people who have lived in it."

"Then if you stay here any length of time it's bound to cheer up."

"That's a sweet thing to say." Impulsively Irena leaned across the seat and kissed him on the cheek. As she started to draw back, Oliver took hold of her shoulders and pulled her against him. He kissed her firmly on the mouth. After a momentary resistance, she relaxed in his arms and responded to the kiss. Oliver felt an almost unbearable desire for this woman building inside him. Without warning she pulled away and fumbled for the door handle.

"I've got to go in."

"Is something wrong?"

"No, I just . . . it's late, that's all."

He reached across her and held the door closed. "No, tell me, did I do something wrong?"

"Oh, no," she said earnestly. "You did everything right. That's the trouble."

"What is that supposed to mean?"

"Nothing. Please let me go in."

Oliver released his grip on the door. Irena pushed it open but made no move to get out.

"Sure you're not angry?" he said.

She gave him the smile again, the one that made him tighten up around the diaphragm. "Don't be silly. I had a marvelous evening. Good dinner, good talk, good company. And I even found a job. If the offer still holds."

"The offer stands," he said. "Come by about ten tomorrow morning."

She pulled his head down and kissed him with surprising vigor. "I'll be there." She stepped out of the cab and hurried up the walk to the gloomy old house.

Oliver sat there until he heard the jingle of her keys, then the opening and closing of the heavy door. He started the engine but stayed where he was for another minute. Quite a woman, this Irena Gallier, he thought. Flirtatious as a kitten one minute, standoffish the next. A familiar pattern with some women, but he didn't think it was calculated with Irena. She was special. She might even be the woman he had been looking for, without even knowing he was looking.

He put the truck in gear and drove away, singing along with an old Beach Boys record on the radio.

Chapter 12

The morning was hot. And humid. It was the kind of a day that happened all too frequently in New Orleans but was not mentioned in the brochures sent out by the tourist bureau.

Even the zoo animals seemed affected by the enervating heat. The usual morning creatures like the birds and the deer sat listlessly regarding the few tourists who had dragged themselves away from their air-conditioned hotel rooms.

One of the few animals unaffected by the weather was the black leopard in the quarantine cage. He prowled restlessly from one side of the cage to the other, glaring all the while at the three people standing outside the bars, talking about him.

Oliver Yates held a clipboard to which was fastened a list of foods, with quantities and frequency of feeding in matching vertical columns. Oliver ticked off the items one by one to Alice Moore, who listened attentively. Behind them Joe Creigh slouched against a tree, hands in his pockets, a cigarette smoldering between his thin lips.

"He's ready to start on a regular feeding schedule now," Oliver said. "One fast day, one light day, then five days' regular food. We want to vary the diet but keep it balanced. You know the usual mix—some viscera, some muscle meat—"

Alice picked it up. "With a few bones now and then, along with the vitamin supplements. Maybe a regular diet will mellow him out."

"Not this one," Joe said, talking around his cigarette. "He's plain mean."

"If an animal is mean," Oliver told him, "you can bet some man is responsible."

Joe took the cigarette out of his mouth, examined the end of it, said nothing.

"I don't suppose I have to tell you," Oliver went on, "that I don't want you in the cage with him again."

"Not freaking likely," Joe said.

"Remember it. You've got a lot to learn about working with animals, Joe, and I think it's too late for you to start with this one."

"That is cool with me. I got a perfectly good T-shirt and a pair of jeans ruined by panther puke."

"I'll see if we can pay for cleaning your clothes out of the budget," Oliver said. "In the meantime, stay away from the cat."

"I heard you the first time," Joe said.

Oliver stared at him for a moment, then turned to Alice. He reached into the pocket of his jacket and pulled out a zip-locked plastic bag. Inside was a dead rat, freshly thawed from the freezer.

"Here's a little treat you can give him. A little extra protein never hurts."

Alice took the bag from him and gazed at it with large green eyes. "Gosh, chief, for a minute I thought it was for me."

"Play your cards right, and I might find another one." Oliver's bantering tone faltered as his eyes strayed up the slope toward the administration building.

Alice and Joe followed his gaze. A slim girl with short brown hair, looking fresh and crisp despite the weather, was just entering the building.

"I'll talk to you later," Oliver said. He tossed the plastic bag containing the dead rat to Alice and strode off along the path toward the administration building.

Alice caught the bag with one hand. "Thanks a lot," she said to Oliver's retreating back. She shaded her eyes against the sun and peered up the slope.

"Who's that girl?" she asked Joe.

"Never saw her before. Maybe she's going to be a new exhibit."

"Very funny." Alice zipped open the bag and took out the rat. There was no squeamishness in the way she handled the dead rodent.

"Here, pussycat," she said, and tossed the rat neatly between the bars into the leopard's cage.

The leopard moved his head swiftly and caught the rat in his mouth the way a dog catches a ball. With the rat's head protruding from one side of his mouth and the tail drooping from the other, the big cat looked at Alice. Then he closed his powerful jaws and pulverized the rat like a peanut.

Oliver was foolishly glad to see the dark-eyed girl. He slowed down and reminded himself to use restraint. After all, they had been together only once, and then not really *together*.

"I'm glad you came," he said.

"I told you I would."

"Do you always do what you say?"

She smiled coquettishly. "Not always."

Oliver laughed. "I'm glad you did this time. Shall we walk over to the gift shop?"

"I wonder . . ." Irena hesitated.

"What?"

"Would it be possible for me to see the leopard?"

"You really like that cat, don't you?"

She nodded.

"His cage is being cleaned right now, it wouldn't be a good time. I'll take you down later, if you like."

"Whatever you say, boss."

Oliver took her arm and they walked together around the long way to the gift shop, by the zoo's main entrance. On the way, Irena asked insightful questions about the animals they passed. Oliver answered with enthusiasm, delighted to find his own interests shared by this girl, who stirred him so deeply in other ways.

Business in the gift shop was slow, as it was everywhere on this soggy day. Oliver led Irena back to a motherly-looking woman who stood by the cash register.

"Irena, this is Mrs. Deever. She manages the place."

"I'm surely glad to have you for as long as you can stay," Mrs. Deever said. "I've been running the place alone since my last girl up and got married on me. You're not planning on getting married, are you?"

"Not right away," Irena said.

She glanced over at Oliver, who blushed like a happy schoolboy.

Although he had other things to do, Oliver walked around the shop with the women as Mrs. Deever showed Irena where the stock was, and how to write up orders and work the cash register. He pretended an interest in all the cups and ashtrays and pennants and other souvenirs bearing the name of the New Orleans Zoo. He watched with pleasure Irena's obvious delight as she handled the cuddly stuffed animals and the ceramic figurines. She only grew serious when she came upon a statuette of a black leopard, jaws wide, teeth bared for attack. She stroked the smooth black head with a forefinger and whispered something only she could hear.

At the quarantine cage Alice completed her daily collection of stool samples. She wondered, not for the first time, if this was any kind of work for a reasonably attractive woman of marriageable age to be doing. It seemed worthwhile when she and Oliver were together, but lately they weren't together nearly enough.

She turned to Joe Creigh. "You can hose out the cage now, but keep the stream of water off the cat. He'll move out of the way if you give him a chance."

"I know the drill," Joe said.

"And I don't have to tell you to stay clear of the bars."

"That's right, you don't have to tell me."

Alice walked down the path toward the patch of woods. Joe stood admiring her rear view until she was out of sight. Damn nice-looking ass. He wondered if Mr. College Man Oliver Yates was getting any of that. Probably. Joe wouldn't mind dipping into it himself. Some time when the two of them were alone he'd make a play. There were plenty of hidden places in the zoo where you could rip off a piece in broad daylight and nobody would ever know.

Joe felt a hard-on growing. He rubbed at it through the rough denim of his pants. There was no two ways about it, he wasn't getting enough gash lately. He wasn't even scoring in the crummy bars where anybody could make out. It was probably the animal stink that he carried home with him from the zoo that was keeping the women away.

He twisted the water-spigot handle and directed a powerful stream from the hose into the leopard's cage. The big cat stood pressed against the bars at the far side of the cage, watching apprehensively as the water sluiced over the floor toward him.

"You've really got it made, you black bastard," Joe told the cat. "You get petted and pampered and taken care of, all you want to eat, a comfortable place to flop, and you never have to do an hour's work."

He moved the stream of water across the floor, inching closer to the leopard.

"They'll probably even find you a she-cat to stick your big black pecker into. You never had it so good."

The leopard eased away from the advancing water along the back wall of the cage, stepping daintily where the cage floor was already wet. Joe gave the hose nozzle a flip, spattering a few drops across the cat's paws.

The sudden thundering roar startled Joe into stumbling backwards, even though the leopard was standing well away from the bars on the near side. The cat raised a paw in Joe's direction and let the deadly claws slide out of their sheaths.

"Don't roar at me, you sonofabitch!" Joe used the stream of water like a whip and lashed it across the broad chest of the leopard.

The big cat reacted with shocking ferocity. With a piercing snarl he sprang across the cage and hit the bars that faced Joe Creigh. Jungle hatred glowed in the hot yellow eyes.

"Don't like the water? Well, that's tough shit, kitty cat, that is plain tough shit."

Joe adjusted the nozzle for the most powerful stream and aimed it directly into the cat's face. The animal shook his big head back and forth, trying to escape the cold water. Joe followed him with the hose.

"Puke on me, will you? Show me your claws? Well, how do you like this, sonofabitch? Maybe from now on you'll show a little respect for Joe Creigh."

The leopard spun frantically, trying to get away from the bedeviling blast of water, but Joe held it on him mercilessly. The cat backed against the rear wall and roared in tormented protest.

In the gift shop Mrs. Deever finished her rundown of the stock for Irena. Oliver was beginning to feel conspicuous hanging around.

He said, "Well, I suppose I'd better be getting back to the office."

Irena walked with him to the door. "I can't thank you enough, Oliver, for getting me the job. And for being so nice to me."

"It doesn't pay a whole lot," he said, "but it's clean work."

"The important thing is I can be near the animals."

From off in the direction of the big cats they heard a wailing roar. Irena turned to Oliver with a look of alarm.

"One of the cats exercising his tonsils." he said.

"No, it's the leopard. He's in some kind of trouble."

Oliver stared at her. "Don't tell me you can already tell the roar of one cat from another."

"The leopard needs help," she said. "I'd better go to him."

It was time to be firm, Oliver decided. He said, "Irena, your job is here in the gift shop. Mine is looking after the animals."

Her gaze flicked beyond him, out the door. "I know, but . . . something is happening to the black leopard."

"I'll go and have a look at him, okay?"

"Yes, please do. And you'll tell me if there's anything wrong?"

"Sure."

A couple with two active children entered the gift shop.

"You have customers," Oliver said. "I'll talk to you later."

As he walked away Irena stood for a moment in the doorway, looking off toward the quarantine cage. When she heard Mrs. Deever clear her throat, she turned reluctantly and went into the shop.

Chapter 13

When Oliver had walked down the path to the quarantine cage and found Joe Creigh tormenting the leopard with the hose, his impulse was to strangle the young man on the spot. However, he got a grip on himself and merely shut off the water. He told Joe to report to his office at noon the next day. That, he reasoned, should give him time to cool off so he would not feel guilty about firing Joe in the heat of the moment.

Now Joe was an hour late, and Oliver was wishing he had thrown him out yesterday when he wanted to. He slumped behind his desk and stared up at a framed print showing a pride of lions majestically taking their ease on a vast African plain. That, he thought, is where animals belong. Free. People too, for that matter.

Another five minutes went by before the door opened and Joe Creigh slouched in. He needed a shave, and he smelled worse than the monkey cage.

"You wanted to see me?" There was an unevenness in the tone of his voice.

"Have you been drinking?" Oliver demanded.

"No," Joe said quickly, but his eyes shifted away from Oliver's.

"Ordinarily that would be enough to finish you here," Oliver said, "but it really doesn't matter, because I'm letting you go anyway."

"What for?" Joe made a try at innocence.

"This kind of work isn't for you, Joe. I hoped you would develop a feeling for the animals, but it hasn't happened. The business with the leopard yesterday was the last straw."

"What do you mean? I was just hosing down his cage. Is it my fault if the sonofabitch got in the way and a little water splashed on him?"

"Cut it out, Joe, I saw you. You deliberately turned the hose on the leopard."

"Well, what of it? After what he did to me—"

"The cat didn't do anything to you that you didn't ask for. I don't want to discuss it any more. Clear the gear out of your locker and get out of here. You'll be paid through the end of the week, but I don't want to see you around here again. And don't forget to turn in your keys."

Joe's face turned a dark, angry red. "Well, fuck you, then, Mister High and Mighty. There are plenty of jobs that pay better than this chickenshit little zoo."

"That's enough," Oliver snapped.

Joe took a step toward him. "Like hell it's enough. There's a few things I want to say to you."

Oliver stood up and pushed the chair back out of the way. His hands balled into fists, and he caught himself hoping the other man would attack. "I've heard all I want to hear from you, Joe. Now get out of here."

For a moment Joe rocked back and forth on the balls of his feet, then the look on Oliver's face seemed to change his mind.

"To hell with you and your freaking animals," he growled, and walked out of the office.

Oliver stood for a moment after he was gone, letting his muscles relax. He was actually disappointed that he had missed the chance to smash Joe Creigh's surly face in. Maybe he *was* spending too much time with the animals.

Down in the basement Joe Creigh slammed his fist against the green-painted locker door. It made a satisfying bang, but it also hurt his fist. He sucked at his bruised knuckles and glared around the deserted locker room.

"The asshole is doing me a favor, that's what," he muttered. "Who wants to spend their life working around a bunch of stinking animals, anyway?"

He sorted through the keys that jangled on a ring at his belt and found the one that opened his locker. He unlocked the door, opened it, and took down the half-pint vodka bottle from the top shelf. The vodka level was down more than half.

Joe raised the bottle toward the ceiling. "Here's to you, Mr. Smartass College-Boy Yates. Fuck you." He brought the bottle to his lips and drank, ending in a coughing fit when some of the liquor was sucked into his windpipe.

When the coughing subsided he recapped the bottle and reached back to stuff it into a hip pocket. However, his coordination was off, and the bottle slipped out of his hand, shattering on the cement floor at his feet.

"Goddamn it!" he swore, and kicked at the wet shards of glass. "This is all that sonofabitch black cat's fault. He's been bad luck for me ever since we brought him in here."

Slowly the fury drained out of Joe's face, to be replaced by an expression of drunken cunning. Okay, so he was fired. No big loss. At least there was nothing more they could do to him now. He might as well give that freaking cat something to really remember him by.

He walked across to the far end of the basement. For a moment he paused before the locked cabinet where the guns were kept for dire emergencies. It was tempting, but he could get in real trouble for that. Besides, the college boy didn't trust anybody else with the keys to the gun cabinet, and he'd have to break in. There was an easier way to even the score with the cat.

He left the guns behind and walked on to the over-sized chest that served as an equipment locker. After trying several of the keys on his ring he found the one that popped open the padlock that secured the lid. He reached inside and poked through the various nets, ropes, snares, and hobbles used when necessary to control the animals. Near the bottom Joe found what he was looking for.

It resembled a long pool cue, except that the tip was copper and the thick end had a rubber hand-grip with a leather loop attached.

Joe unscrewed the butt end and looked in to see that the batteries were in place. But were they still good? Since the college boy had been in charge, use of the electric prod was forbidden. Joe screwed the butt back on, held the rubber hand grip, and brought the copper tip to within a half inch of the metal locker. He pressed the trigger button. A satisfying spark jumped from the tip of the prod to the locker.

Joe laughed aloud. "Oh, *yeah!* You're in for a shock, pussycat." He laughed all the louder at his joke. "Yes, you sonofabitch, you're going to remember Joe Creigh."

Taking care to slip out of the building unseen, Joe made his way down the bank and into the clump of trees. He carried the electric prod out in front of him with both hands, like a rifle. His flesh tingled with excitement. It was too bad he hadn't thought of this a long time ago. The leopard was not the only animal in the zoo he would like to hurt. But the leopard was the worst of the lot. He was the one who had puked on Joe, cost him his job. Yes, by God, the black sonofabitch was going to pay today.

The leopard lay dozing on its shelf-bed when Joe approached the quarantine cage. Joe smiled, his eyes bright with anticipation.

"Taking a little nap, are you, you lazy bastard? A little catnap?"

Joe giggled as he moved up close to the bars. He clapped a hand over his mouth. It would not do to wake the cat up before he was ready.

He looped the leather strap around his wrist, then slowly and carefully he poked the electric prod between the bars, the tip moving toward the sleeping leopard.

"Easy now, easy," he told himself in a whisper. "Don't spoil the surprise."

The copper tip of the prod hovered just over the leopard's glossy flank, just a handspan away from its fur.

"Now!" Joe stabbed the tip of the prod against the animal's side and punched the electrifying trigger button.

There was a short sizzling sound, and the leopard went straight up into the air with a startled scream. It landed on all fours in the center of the cage and looked around with hurt, bewildered eyes.

Joe Creigh slapped the side of his leg and laughed. Damned if that wasn't the funniest thing he ever saw. It was sure as hell worth getting fired for.

The leopard saw him. The puzzled look went out of the flat yellow eyes, to be replaced by a smoldering hatred.

"How about that, nigger cat? You want some more?"

The leopard snarled, showing Joe the killer teeth.

"You don't scare me. Not with those bars between us." He lunged like a fencer, hitting the trigger button as the tip of the prod touched the cat's face.

The leopard howled and sprang back to the far side of the cage. He used one big paw to rub at his nose where the spark had burned him.

Oh, this was just too good. That black sonofabitch

was scared shitless. Joe could not remember when he had felt so good. He was even getting a hard-on.

He moved around the outside of the cage to a spot closer to the leopard. "You can't get away from me," he said. "There's no place in that cage where I can't get at you."

To prove it he lunged out with the prod again and shocked the cat in the center of his powerful chest. The leopard howled again and spun away along the back wall of the cage.

Joe moved along the front bars until he and the animal were directly across from each other. "I told you you can't get away from me. You know, I wonder what would happen if I stuck this thing right in your ear."

The leopard crouched, not moving. The black lips pulled back into grin of primeval rage. Joe reached in through the bars, probing for one of the cat's small, laidback ears.

Faster than the eye could follow, the cat's jaws snapped, and suddenly he had the electric prod clamped between his killer teeth. He held it at the middle, where the electrified tip was harmless to him.

"What the hell?" Joe got out. He released the hand grip and tried to free his wrist from the tough leather strap. He was not fast enough. With a toss of his head, the leopard jerked on the prod, dragging Joe up against the bars, immobile, with his arm fully extended inside the cage.

For a moment that seemed like an eternity, Joe stood with his face pressed against the steel, looking into those yellow, hate-filled eyes. Neither the man nor the animal moved. Joe's right arm began to ache. He smelled the stink of his own fear. He opened his mouth to shout for help, but before the cry could pass his lips, the leopard released the prod and sank the killer teeth into Joe Creigh's arm.

Chapter 14

The sound of the man's scream jolted Oliver out of his chair and sent him running for the door. The scream had come from the direction of the quarantine cage. Oliver did not want to speculate on what was happening down there.

He bolted out of his office and down the hall toward the side entrance to the building. As he turned for the door he almost collided with Alice Moore, running from the opposite direction.

"What is it?" she cried.

"I don't know. It came from the leopard's cage."

Without wasting more words Oliver ran out through the door and down the slope toward the trees. Alice followed him.

In the gift shop, farther away from the quarantine cage, Irena also heard the man's scream. She looked up and gasped.

Mrs. Deever, who was laying out a fresh supply of *Born Free* T-shirts, looked over at her.

"What is it, Irena?"

"Didn't you hear that?"

"Hear what?"

As the man's scream died, a sound reached Irena's ears that was even more chilling. It was the low, triumphant growl of a cat that has caught its prey.

"I've got to go to him." Irena moved toward the door.

Mrs. Deever started after her. The older woman's face was creased with concern. "Irena, what's the matter?"

"I—I'm sorry," Irena said, and fled out of the shop, leaving the little bell on a spring over the door tinkling behind her.

As Oliver burst out of the trees and onto the clearing before the quarantine cage, he froze. Joe Creigh was jammed up tight against the bars on the outside. Inside, the black leopard sat, looking quite calm, with his jaws clamped on Joe's arm at the elbow.

"My God!" Oliver breathed.

Joe turned his head as far as he could manage and looked at him. The young man's face was waxen with pain and incipient shock.

"Help me!" His voice was hoarse and barely recognizable. "Help me!"

Alice came running up beside Oliver and stopped suddenly. "Jesus, the cat's got him!"

"Stay here," Oliver said under his breath. He started toward the cage, moving slowly, keeping his hands in sight so he would not alarm the leopard. The big cat watched his approach intently, the yellow eyes bright.

"Take it easy now," Oliver said. "Just take it easy." He was talking as much to Joe Creigh, obviously on the brink of panic, as he was to the leopard.

When he came to within six feet of the cage Oliver saw the electric prod lying inside on the floor and deduced what had happened.

"Shit," he said to himself, and took another step toward the cage. The leopard growled softly and bit down a little harder on Joe's arm.

The young handler squealed in pain. The front of his denim pants darkened, and a pool of urine spread at his feet.

Alice had moved up cautiously behind Oliver on the grass. "What can we do?" she whispered.

"Go get the tranq gun out of the truck," Oliver said. "I'll try to keep things together here."

As though the cat had understood his words, he began backing away toward the center of the cage, with Joe's arm still firmly clenched between his teeth.

"Oh my God, it hurts," Joe moaned. "Make him let go of me."

"Oh!"

Oliver turned at the sound of the new voice. Irena was standing at the head of the path that led off toward the zoo proper.

"What are you doing here?" he said.

"I heard the leopard." Irena's eyes were huge, watching the cat with the man's arm in its mouth.

The leopard gave its head a jerk. It was just a tiny movement, but it brought popping noises from Joe's armpit.

"Oh, Jesus, no no *no!*" Joe screamed.

Oliver could not wait for Alice to come back with the tranquilizer rifle. The big cat was going to destroy the man's arm. Oliver sprang forward, wrapped his arms around Joe's waist, and fell backward, hoping to jerk the other man free of the bars as he had Irena the night he found her here.

The leopard responded by crunching down on Joe's elbow and pulling harder into the cage. Oliver knew he could not hope to win a tug-of-war with the powerful beast.

He let go of Joe, who was now slobbering incoherently, and ran back behind the cage. There, in a wooden box bolted to the outside cage wall, was a carbon-dioxide fire extinguisher. Oliver had talked Bronte Judson into installing a dozen of them around the zoo just six months before. He snatched the extinguisher free of the spring clips that held it and prayed that the CO_2 cartridge still held its charge.

When Oliver raced back to the open side of the cage, the leopard was standing with all four feet braced, worrying the arm with savage shakes of its head. The floor of the cage was spattered with blood. Joe Creigh stood squeezed against the bars, grunting with agony every time the cat jerked his arm.

Oliver moved along the bars until he had a clear shot at the cat, shoved the black nozzle of the extinguisher into the cage, and hit the trigger. A cloud of white smoke billowed into the cage. Under the hiss of the CO_2 Oliver could hear a thick tearing, cracking sound.

Joe Creigh stumbled backwards, his face greasy white. His left arm flapped wildly in the air. His right arm was not there any more.

Oliver cut off the CO_2 and started toward Joe. The young man whirled on the grass in a wild dance of pain, blood spurting like a crimson fountain from the ragged, empty shoulder socket.

Alice came running out of the woods carrying the tranquilizer gun. When she saw Joe, she dropped the rifle and turned almost as pale as he was.

When the cloud of gas dissipated in the cage they saw the black leopard sitting in the center of the floor, shaking its great head back and forth. The two ends of Joe Creigh's right arm flopped at either side of the cat's mouth as the bone and muscle were ground into a pulp by the cruel teeth.

Joe Creigh at last stopped his demented jig and fell heavily to the ground. Mercifully, he lost consciousness as blood continued to pump from the severed brachial artery.

Oliver ran to the side of the fallen man, pausing long enough to grab Alice by the arm and shake her back to her senses. Her eyes cleared gradually and she looked to him for instructions.

"Get to a telephone," he said. "Call for paramedics. An ambulance."

"It's too late," Irena said quietly.

Oliver's head jerked around. He had forgotten for a moment that she was there. Irena was standing several feet away. A stream of blood from Joe's torn shoulder had run down to form a puddle at her feet. Her white shoes were stained with crimson.

"What do you mean, too late?" Oliver said.

"You can't do anything for him. He's dying."

Oliver looked down at the slack gray face of the young man. The flow of blood was already lessening as the body emptied itself of fluids. Joe's eyes were open, the pupils rolled back up into his head.

"We've still got to do what we can," Oliver said.

When he looked up again Irena was staring into the cage. There, with the ragged remains of the man's arm in its mouth, the cat stared back at her.

Chapter 15

Oliver was prepared to wait at the hospital until there was definitive word on Joe Creigh's condition, but the hospital staff made it clear that he would only be in the way, and the outcome of the surgery might not be known for many hours. He took Alice home after they gave her a sedative at the hospital. Irena had slipped away after the violent events of the afternoon, and Oliver had not had time to try to reach her.

He sat later with a grim-faced Bronte Judson in his poorly lighted office, listening to the sounds of the night creatures. To Oliver it seemed that every animal in the zoo was awake and restless tonight. He could identify most of the cries and squawks and chitterings, but there were other voices that were strange to him. Sitting stiff and frowning across the desk from him, Bronte Judson paid no attention to the animals. He had other problems.

The telephone on the desk pealed, and both men jumped as though they had been shot. Oliver snatched up the instrument and barked a "Yes?" into the mouthpiece.

He sat with his lips pressed together in a grim line as he heard from the other end of the line the report he had been dreading. He hung up the phone without saying goodbye.

"Well?" Judson demanded.

"That was the hospital," Oliver said in a distracted tone.

"Of course it was the hospital. Who else would be calling here tonight? What did they say?"

"Joe Creigh is dead."

Judson groaned. "Oh Lord, the city inspectors are going to be all over us now. There might even be a grand jury convened."

"He never really had a chance," Oliver went on. "He was in deep shock by the time they got him to the hospital, and with all the blood he lost, they just couldn't save him."

"I'll probably be called in by the mayor for an explanation," Judson said. "What am I going to tell him?"

"If we had better medical facilities on the grounds, we might have done more for him."

"And the budget. What's going to happen to our budget when the council convenes?"

Oliver stared across the desk at the chief administrator. "Screw the budget."

"Sure, that's easy for you to say. You've got all those big-money offers from the colleges to fall back on. If this zoo goes under I'm out of a job."

Oliver spoke slowly and distinctly. "Bronte, a man is dead."

"I know, I know, and I feel as badly about it as you do. I'll tell you one thing for sure—that cat is gone."

"What do you mean, *gone?*"

"I mean there is one thing I am going to be able to tell the mayor or the grand jury or whoever, and that is that we will not tolerate a killer animal in the New Orleans Zoo."

"It wasn't the leopard's fault."

"Don't start your Humane Society pitch with me, Oliver. That leopard killed a man."

"The man was tormenting him with an electric prod."

"What's that got to do with it?"

"A lot, I'd say. You can't expect an animal to take that kind of mistreatment."

"There's no point in discussing this any further," Judson said. "The cat is gone."

"Explain that."

"Back when you told me what an unusual animal it was, the size and all, I shopped it around a little. I got one really good offer from Cromartie Labs, in Houston. Today I accepted it."

Oliver jumped to his feet. "Cromartie Labs? Those people are butchers. Worse! You know what they'll do? They'll pull that leopard apart, piece by piece, while he's still alive and feeling. I won't allow any of my animals to be turned over to those torturers."

"It's out of your hands, Oliver. The deal is made. Not only will it get this killer off our hands, we stand to make a few bucks on the deal."

"Make a few bucks? Bronte, don't you have any heart?"

"Yes, I have," the administrator said quietly. "You might think back and remember that I suggested in the beginning that painless euthanasia might be the best way to go."

"I couldn't have killed the animal without a reason."

"Well, now there's a reason."

Judson stood up and adjusted the crease in his trousers. "I'll have to start putting together some kind of release for the media. Is there anything you want me to say?"

Oliver sagged back into his chair. "No."

"Good night, then," Judson said. "Keep your fingers crossed that we don't come out of this too badly."

Once the administrator was gone, Oliver sat for a long time staring down at the coffee-stained blotter pad on his desk. The night voices spoke to him.

Cromartie Labs. The damned sadists should have

been put out of business long ago. Oliver ground his teeth, visualizing the agony the leopard would be put through before death finally came.

"I can't let it happen," he said to the empty office.

Oliver left the room, walked through the deserted building, and down the stairs to the basement. He went to the gun cabinet and opened it with his key. From the small selection of rifles and handguns inside, he picked a reliable Winchester bolt-action model. He loaded it with steel-jacketed 300 Magnum cartridges. He picked up a heavy flashlight, climbed the stairs from the basement, and went out of the building.

The loaded rifle weighed like a cannon when Oliver carried it out into the night and down the slope toward the trees. The sounds of the animals were all around him. Never in his life had he felt so alone.

With the flashlight beam picking out the trail ahead of him, he made his way through the grove of trees and out onto the patch of level grass that surrounded the quarantine cage. Everything looked so calm in the moonlight, a sharp contrast to the wild scene of a few hours before.

He snapped off the flashlight and walked softly around toward the front of the cage. There was no sense alarming the cat too soon. Also, Oliver admitted to himself, he was in no hurry to look into the eyes of the creature he was about to kill.

He found a grassy spot in front of the cage and knelt there. It was too dark to see anything inside, but from there he would have a clear shot at the cat, wherever it happened to be. He worked the bolt, levering a cartridge up into the chamber. It made a loud clacking sound in the night air.

"Sorry, big fella," Oliver said softly, "but this is the way it has to be. I will not let them rip you apart in Houston."

He thumbed on the flashlight, ready to bring the rifle into play immediately and swept the interior of the cage with the beam of light.

The leopard was not inside.

Incredulous, Oliver rose to his feet and walked closer to the bars. He played the light over every inch of the cage interior—the floor, the shelf, all four corners.

The leopard was not inside.

Feeling a sudden chill between his shoulder blades, Oliver whirled and swept the surrounding brush with the flashlight beam. Tiny eyes glittered back at him, and little feet scurried away over the dried leaves, but there was no leopard.

Moving cautiously, the rifle held ready for use, he advanced to the door of the cage. With the flashlight clamped awkwardly under one arm, he fumbled for the key that would open the cage door. He found it and started to insert it into the lock. At the slight pressure the door swung inward.

The cage was unlocked.

Oliver stood holding the key while his mind raced. How could such a thing have happened? After the tragedy here earlier, he had personally tested the cage to be sure it was sound. There was no doubt that the door was locked then. It was sure as hell open now.

He stepped into the cage, holding the flashlight before him. There was something on the floor, back by the rear wall. The cage had been thoroughly hosed out after the leopard's attack on Joe today, but something was lying there.

Oliver walked closer, bending down to see better what was on the floor. There was a pool of thick grayish mucus. In the center of the pool was something that looked like a fragment of dark, decaying flesh.

Oliver nudged the shapless lump with the toe of his

boot. The sticky resilience made him shudder. It was definitely not feces, but what the devil could it be?

Abruptly he turned away. There was much to do. Somewhere loose in the night was a deadly animal. It was no longer in Oliver's hands. The police would have to be called. He would want Alice to help him. This was going to be a very long night.

Chapter 16

Irena sat on the edge of the bed in her room at the Gallier house and stared down at the white shoes, which still rested where she had stepped out of them. They were still spotted with Joe Creigh's blood. Since arriving home late this afternoon, she had consciously shut out of her mind the horrifying scene at the zoo. She had spoken briefly to Femolly, taken a shower, put on a long satin nightgown, and climbed into bed. However, she did not sleep.

Now, staring at the blood spots, brown and crusted on the white leather, she could no longer pretend that nothing had happened. Impulsively she kicked the shoes across the room, where they thumped against the wall. That stupid young man! Why did he have to torment the leopard into an act of violence?

She picked up her sketchbook from the bedside table and began to leaf through it, critically studying the pages that were filled with drawings of the big cat.

"You poor lovely creature," she said. "What will happen to you now? Who will protect you? Who will give you love?"

With a sudden crash the door leading to the balcony burst open. Irena stifled a cry as a man stepped into the room.

"Paul!"

Her brother stood for a moment framed by the black night outside the window. He was pale, with a stubble of beard. His eyes had a wild, unnatural glitter.

"Where have you been?"

"I was . . . in prison," he said haltingly.

"Prison? I don't understand."

"The convicts. They need spiritual help as much as those of us on the outside. Perhaps more. I spend time with them whenever I can."

"You left so suddenly."

"I had no choice. There was a boy who was dying. He asked for me. I'm sorry I had no time to say goodbye."

Irena went to her brother and wrapped her arms around him. "You're here now, that's what matters. Oh, Paul, I've had such a terrible day."

From out in the night came the distant braying of a police siren. Paul eased out of Irena's embrace and turned to close the window.

Irena stepped back and looked at him more closely. "What is it, Paul? You seem so strange."

"Do I?" His voice was taut. Different-sounding. He crossed the room, turned the key in the bedroom door, and pocketed it.

"What are you doing?" Irena said.

He looked at her with a smile she had never seen before. "When you came here, I didn't know if you were ready. I didn't want to do anything too soon, so I waited. But now, I've seen how you are about him, and I know you are ready."

"I don't know what you're talking about. How I am about who?"

"The zoo keeper, of course." Paul spat the words out.

"You're not making sense, Paul."

"I'll spell it out for you. You want to fuck the zoo keeper, don't you."

The word hit her like a slap across the face. Irena recoiled.

"Don't bother to deny it. I could smell it on you. Wanting to fuck him. And do other things too. It burns you up, the wanting. You can taste him in your mouth, feel him in your cunt. Yes, it makes you burn. You're burning now, aren't you, little sister?"

He started toward her. Irena shrank away.

"No! Stay away from me! Don't touch me!"

"Don't you see, I'm the only one who *can* touch you. And you're the only one who can touch me. We're safe together, because we're alike."

"I'm *not* like you. You're sick!"

"Oh, yes, you are. We are the same, little sister. You know we are. You've always known it. Don't you remember when we were children? When you were just a little girl? How you and I heard voices and knew things that other people can't possibly know?"

The sirens in the night grew louder. Now there was the barking of dogs in the distance.

"Paul, you're really in trouble. You need help."

"That's not what I need, little sister. I need the same thing you do. And tonight we are going to nourish each other."

He sprang forward and seized her so swiftly that she had no time to react. He spun her around and pinned both arms behind her back, holding them at the wrists with one powerful hand. Irena struggled, but it was useless against her brother's strength. He marched her toward the bed.

"Paul, please don't do this," she cried. "Don't hurt me."

"Don't you understand, I have to? You and I are the same blood, Irena. We need each other. We need each other's bodies."

He pushed her forward until her knees bumped against the edge of the bed. His free hand hit her in the small of the back and she fell face forward across the bed. Paul released her wrists but kept one hand flat against her back, pressing her down onto the bed. She tried to cry out, but her voice was muffled by the blankets.

"Struggle as much as you like," he said. "You can't stop what's going to happen to you. You don't really want to stop it, do you, Irena?"

She felt him grasp the hem of her nightgown. He pulled it up, and the chill of the night air hit her bare buttocks. His fingers probed and pinched at the tender flesh.

"You've never done it before, have you?" he said, breathing hard.

"No . . . never! Please, Paul, don't do this."

"You don't know how lucky you are that I will be your first lover. One of your own. When it is over, you will thank me."

His hand slipped down the crease of her rump and insinuated itself up tight between her legs. In spite of her revulsion, Irena felt herself go moist down there.

"You see?" Paul said close to her ear. "You do want me to do it. You need it as much as I do."

He grasped the backs of her thighs, his fingers digging into the firm flesh, and forced her legs apart. She felt him move in between her spread legs, felt his hard penis rub against her flesh.

With all the strength she could summon, Irena twisted and writhed from side to side.

"Damn you, hold still," Paul growled.

She thrashed around even harder, then screamed suddenly as Paul's teeth sank into the skin on the back of her neck. She snapped her head backwards and felt the back of her skull crack against her brother's forehead. He grunted and lost his grip on her, staggering back a step.

Irena sprang off the bed and whirled to face this madman who was her brother. There was a smear of

135

blood on his mouth. Her blood. He shook himself and started toward her.

Instinctively Irena slashed out at his face with clawed fingers. Her nails dug in and raked red furrows down the flesh of his cheek.

Paul reached up and touched the deep scratches. He smiled.

"You see?" he said, and started toward her again.

Irena spun away and ran for the window. She snatched it open and stumbled out onto the balcony. Breathing raggedly, Paul lurched after her.

Outside the sound of the sirens was very close. The dogs too. They seemed to be right in the neighborhood.

Irena edged sideways along the balcony with her back against the iron railing, her eyes never leaving Paul as he came after her. He lunged, reaching for her. She danced away, avoiding his grasp, but her foot slipped on a damp spot. She fell against the railing, fought for a moment for her balance, and toppled over.

Falling.

Like the terrifying childhood dream where the ground rushes up at incredible speed. The wind roared in Irena's ears as she waited for the impact that would crack her bones and smash her internal organs.

But the impact never came. Somehow her body twisted in midair so she landed on the lawn below, hitting on all fours, cushioning the shock. She bounced immediately to her feet as she heard Paul hit the ground close to her.

She was running then, down the path to the tall iron gate, through the gate, and out onto the street. Running, running, with the sound of Paul's footfalls behind her pounding ever closer.

There were sudden blinding lights and a confusion of sounds as Irena ran on in blind panic. Her only thought was to escape the beast that had been her brother. Her eyes streamed with tears as she ran on, heedless of anything in her path.

It was the screech of tires that finally stopped her. A pair of headlights dipped and bounced, almost touching her as the driver brought the car to a tortured stop.

A door slammed. There was a new set of footsteps, and Irena was held in a strong pair of arms. Not like Paul's terrible embrace, these were loving and protective. She pressed her face into the rough material of the man's jacket and began to sob.

"Irena," Oliver said, holding the shaking girl close against him. "Irena, darling, what happened?"

Chapter 17

It was several minutes before Irena could catch her breath and talk coherently. Oliver's arms around her were strong and protective. She did not want him to take them away.

"It's all right," he said soothingly, his lips close to her ear. "Just take your time. There's nothing to be afraid of now."

Standing back behind Oliver in the glow of the headlights, Irena could see Alice Moore. The redheaded woman was watching her carefully.

"It was my brother, Paul," Irena said when she regained some of her control. "I don't know what happened to him. He seemed to go crazy. He ... he attacked me. I got out of the house and ran. Paul chased me. He kept getting closer. And then suddenly you were there."

Oliver looked around in the darkness. "There's no sign of him now."

A police car screeched to a stop in the street next to them. Reluctantly Irena moved out of Oliver's arms as he turned to greet Sergeant Brant.

"Is the girl all right?" asked the big detective.

"Yes," Oliver said. "Just frightened. Her brother seems to have had an attack of some kind. What about the leopard?"

"We tracked him to the Gallier house. The dogs are outside now, going crazy. I'd like your permission to go in, Miss Gallier."

"Y—yes, of course," Irena said. "Anything you have to do."

Brant nodded to them and jogged off up the street. "Let's go in," he called to the waiting policemen. "Be careful, and keep a tight hold on the dogs."

Oliver looked off toward the house, now bathed in spotlights from the police cars. "Do you feel well enough to go back there?" he asked Irena.

"Maybe she ought to wait in the truck," Alice said.

"Oh, no, I'm all right now," Irena said quickly. "I have to know what they find."

They started back toward the house. Oliver took Irena's arm protectively. Alice followed a few paces behind, saying nothing.

The lights were all blazing when they entered the house. Femolly was in the dining room, sitting in a straight-back chair while a detective questioned her. The dogs could be heard barking urgently in the kitchen.

"I was asleep the whole time," Femolly told the detective.

"You didn't hear anything?"

"Nothin', till you people came banging on the door with your dogs barking and all." The dark woman looked up when Irena came into the room. There was a strange combination of sorrow and relief in her expression.

Sergeant Brant entered through the swinging door leading from the kitchen. He took Oliver discreetly aside. "Will you and Miss Moore come with me for a minute? There's something I want you to see."

Oliver glanced over at Irena.

"I'll have a man stay with her," Brant said.

Oliver signaled to Alice, and they followed the detective through the kitchen to a door that was partly hidden behind a big refrigerator. A heavy padlock dangled from a hasp. The screws that held the hasp to the door frame had been pried out of the wood.

Oliver looked questioningly at Brant.

"We had Miss Gallier's permission," said the policeman.

With Brant in the lead they picked their way down a crumbling flight of stone steps into the basement. The air was cold and damp. Tomblike. They had to duck their heads to avoid a maze of corroded pipes overhead as they crossed the damp, uneven floor. Ahead of them a uniformed policeman stood in a pool of yellow light from a dangling overhead bulb. The policeman was holding a handkerchief to his nose.

As they picked their way across the basement, Oliver recognized the smell. Dead flesh. Some of it dead a long time. As they came closer to the policeman they could make out a caged-off corner of the basement. Steel bars extended from the heavy ceiling beams to the concrete floor.

"I think we've found where your leopard came from," Sergeant Brant said.

Oliver and Alice went closer and looked through the bars into the cage. It was filthy inside. Animal feces, bones, and strange bits of withered flesh littered the floor. A stout chain was bolted to one wall. The other end was attached to a thick metal collar.

"What a terrible way to keep an animal," Alice said.

Oliver bent over and examined the collar. "This is rusted shut," he said. "It hasn't been used in a long time."

"Maybe the collar hasn't," said Brant, "but something has sure as hell been using this cage."

Alice reached in through the bars to poke at a large yellowed bone. "At least the animal was fed."

"I wouldn't touch that, Miss Moore," said Brant. "It's human remains."

"Are you sure?" Oliver asked.

The detective nodded. "There are human skulls in

the far corner. From the looks of it there's parts of three, maybe four, bodies in there. Wouldn't surprise me if we found others buried on the grounds."

"What the devil was going on here?" Oliver asked.

"Off the record, it looks like this Paul Gallier has been killing people and feeding them to the cat. There's been a few we've found—prostitutes, female runaways, and the like. Half eaten. Mutilated, especially in the genital area."

Alice cleared her throat.

"Sorry, Miss Moore."

Alice waved away the apology.

"What could make a man do a thing like that?" Oliver said.

"Who knows? The housekeeper says he's been in and out of psycho wards since he was a kid. He's also some kind of a religious nut.

"But the leopard," Alice said, "where would he get that? How did he learn to handle it?"

"He was raised around them. His parents were circus people. Lion trainers. They weren't exactly your apple-pie mom and dad, either. He caught her in bed with another man one day, shot her dead, then blew his brains out."

"What about his sister?" Alice asked. "Is she involved in this?"

"How could she be?" Oliver said. "Irena hadn't seen her brother in years until a week ago. Tonight we found her running on the street after he tried to attack her."

"I'll want to hear more about that," Brant said. "At the moment we have no reason to suspect her. It seems likely the brother was planning to kill her too. If she's a friend of yours, you ought to suggest that she find another place to live."

"I'll take care of that," Oliver said.

Alice shot him a look, which he ignored.

"Good. That leaves us with a couple of problems. One, we got a leopard loose out there somewhere, and he likes human flesh."

"You mean a leopard that was *trained* to eat human flesh," Oliver corrected.

"Doesn't make a whole lot of difference, the way I see it. The second problem we got is the maniac who trained the cat. Let's go upstairs."

Femolly, wearing her coat, stood in the doorway. A policeman standing beside her had his hand lightly but firmly on her arm.

Irena ran to Sergeant Brant when he came into the room with Oliver and Alice.

"Do you have to arrest Femolly? She hasn't done anything."

"I'm sorry, Miss Gallier," the detective said, "but at the very least we have to hold her as a material witness. She had to have knowledge of what was going on here."

Irena walked over to the proud black woman and touched her hand. "Femolly, is there anything I can do?"

"Don't you worry none about me, child. You just take care of yourself. You got lots bigger things to be worrying about."

Brant gave a signal, and the policeman led Femolly out of the house. To Oliver he said, "You were going to arrange a place for Miss Gallier to stay?"

"I have an extra room at my house. She can stay there." He turned to Irena. "If that's all right with you."

"Oliver!" Alice's voice was sharp.

He turned to her impatiently. "What is it?"

"Do you think this is a good idea?"

"She certainly can't stay here, and she doesn't know anybody else in New Orleans."

"Please, I don't want to be any trouble," Irena said.

"No trouble," Oliver assured her. "You're welcome to stay at my place until we can work something else out. Until they find your brother, anyway." He turned to look at Alice. "Unless you have a better idea."

"Put her wherever you want to," Alice said.

Oliver regarded her for a moment, then returned to Irena. "Do you have much to pack?"

"Just a few things."

"I'll wait down here for you. Alice will go along and help you pack. Won't you, Alice?"

"Sure," Alice said without enthusiasm. "Lead the way."

Oliver watched the two women go up the stairs. Irena looked back at him over her shoulder. A fleeting smile touched the corners of her mouth. At that moment he knew he was falling in love with her.

Chapter 18

Irena stood in the center of Oliver's compact living room and looked around. "It's lovely."

"It used to be a carriage house," Oliver told her. "The rooms upstairs were for the servants. It's sort of a converted garage."

"They don't make garages like they used to," Irena said.

"Nor anything else."

"Oliver?"

"Yes?"

"Alice wasn't very happy about you bringing me here, was she?"

"Alice is . . . well, she's just being a woman."

"Are you and she . . . ?"

"No, nothing like that," he said quickly. "We're good friends. We work together."

"I got the feeling Alice thinks there's something more."

"I can't help that. Maybe she thought I was bringing you here to throw you into the sack and ravish you." He put on a grin to show he was kidding.

"Were you?" Irena's eyes remained serious.

Oliver's grin faded. "That wasn't my purpose. If you want to know if I'm attracted to you, the answer is yes. But I don't take women to bed under false pretenses."

"I'm glad to hear that. I'm a virgin, you know."

Oliver looked embarrassed. "No, I didn't."

"Does it make any difference in the way you feel about me?"

"Why should it?"

"I don't know. These days, if you're still a virgin at twenty-one, people think there's something wrong with you."

Oliver came over and put his arms around her. He held her tenderly for a moment, then kissed her on the cheek. "As far as I've been able to tell, there is absolutely nothing wrong with you. If anything, I'm even more attracted to you now."

She smiled up at him. "I think I needed to hear that."

He let her go and took a step back. "What the hell are we talking about? You were almost killed tonight. There's a sick man and a dangerous cat loose in the streets. This is no time to talk romance. Come on, I'll show you your room." He picked up her bag and started toward the stairs.

"Oliver?"

He turned back to look at her.

"I don't expect to still be a virgin at twenty-two."

He held a severe expression for a moment, then broke into a grin. "Come on, you, upstairs. I've got to grab a couple of hours' sleep. I promised Brant I'd help him look for the leopard first thing in the morning."

Irena stopped before a glassed-in bookcase at the foot of the stairs. The books had been disarranged to make room for a heavy-caliber rifle.

"You're not a hunter?" she said.

Oliver turned on the stairway. "The rifle? No, I brought that home from the zoo earlier today. I just stuck it in there to get it out of the way until I take it back."

"I'm glad," Irena said. "I don't like people who kill for sport."

"Neither do I," Oliver said.

For a moment their eyes held, then he continued up the stairs. Irena followed him to a comfortable-looking room, simply furnished, with a large window that looked out on trees in the back yard. Oliver set her bag down on the floor at the foot of the bed.

"If you need me for anything, my room is right next door."

Irena shuddered, suddenly remembering the ugly events earlier in the evening.

Oliver saw the change in her expression. "Don't worry, Irena, they'll find Paul."

Her eyes were clouded. "I can't believe he did all those things the police say he did. Not my brother."

"He's not responsible," Oliver said gently. "He needs help. He'll get it when they find him." He stood in the doorway for a moment longer but saw that Irena was off somewhere in her own thoughts.

"Good night," he said. "I'll probably be out by the time you get up. Just make yourself at home."

When she was alone Irena began to undress. She pulled off the blouse she had hastily donned at the Gallier house and stood with her back to the mirror that hung over the bureau. By turning her head she could just see the marks of teeth where Paul had clamped onto the back of her neck. She touched the wound, found the sensation strangely pleasurable. Quickly she slipped off the rest of her clothes, turned out the lights, and got into bed.

Sleep did not come easily. The unfamiliar bed, the strange sounds inside and outside the house, the terrible events of the day, combined to keep Irena awake long past midnight.

When at last she did sleep, her dreams were worse than her waking fears. She was walking alone in a strange land where desert met jungle. In the distance loomed cool, misty mountains. It seemed to be night, yet Irena's vision in the dream was as keen as at midday.

Some force drew her on towards the jungle. Some-

146

thing there was calling her name. As she approached, moving effortlessly over the dream landscape, she could make out a standing figure at the edge of the jungle. A man. He beckoned her on. Irena felt a mixture of repulsion and desire. She floated toward the beckoning figure, unable to resist.

When she was almost close enough to make out his features, the dark figure moved back deeper into the jungle. Irena had no choice but to follow.

The thick, moist brush closed in around her. Up ahead one tree stood out from the rest. Its trunk was gnarled and twisted as though it writhed in agony. The branches spread a dark canopy that shut out the dream sky. The silent figure stood waiting for her at the base of the tree. It was Paul.

He was naked. His tall, sinewy body seemed to glow with a soft inner light. Irena saw his nakedness in every detail. Desire burned within her even as a voice in her head screamed *No! This is wrong!*

She glided toward him. Her own body yearned to join with his. Paul held out his arms to her. Irena could feel the heat of him. Then she looked up into his face. It was the face of a cat.

Irena gasped. The sudden rush of air into her lungs awakened her. She looked about wildly for a moment, disoriented. She was not in her bed. She was standing, naked, in a strange room. On a bed before her, his body only partially covered by a sheet, lay Oliver Yates.

Shocked, Irena started to back away, but something held her where she stood. The hot desire she had known in the dream returned. She felt the dampness between her legs, and touched herself there.

Oliver stirred in his sleep, making a small sound. He rolled over and the sheet fell away completely. Irena devoured his body with her eyes. She longed to stroke his flesh, caress him, taste him.

She had no feeling for the passage of time as she stood there. Only the gray streaks of dawn at the window brought her back to the moment.

Silently she slipped out of Oliver's room and returned to her own. She got into bed and stroked the place where her thighs joined, until she fell at last into a dreamless sleep.

Chapter 19

Irena awoke to a lovely, sun-bright day. The dreams of the night before, along with the embarrassing sleepwalking episode, were washed away by the fresh breeze that stirred the curtains and cooled her room.

She showered long and thoroughly, rubbing her skin pink with one of a stack of fluffy towels she found in the bathroom. She hoped Oliver would return before too long. She was anxious to hear his voice, see him smile.

She dressed quickly, packed her things away in drawers, and went downstairs. Feeling a little bit naughty, she prowled around the living room, looking at Oliver's things, touching some of them. It was a completely masculine room, but in no way cold. The colors were earth tones, the furniture comfortable. The place was reasonably clean, for a bachelor.

There were plants growing in sturdy pots around the room. That was unusual for a man living alone, but these were big, masculine plants, not the dainty little things some women talked to like babies. One wall was given over to framed photographs. Irena crossed the room for a closer look.

Most of the pictures were of animals, taken in their natural habitat. There were shots of Oliver in safari jacket and boots, looking very handsome. Often he was standing with native tribesmen. Africa? South America? Irena could not be sure.

There were pictures of Oliver and Alice Moore together. Apparently she accompanied him on at least some of the expeditions. In one of the photos they had their arms around each other and smiled happily out at the camera. Just good friends?

Irena felt a pang of jealousy. Why? Surely she did not think Oliver had never been with another woman? Why did it bother her to see him in such a familiar pose with his coworker? After all, she was the one living in his house now, not Alice Moore.

A small sound from another part of the house distracted her from the photographs. She turned her head to listen. There was a metallic rattling, then a squawk.

Irena followed the sound into the small kitchen. A birdcage hung in the window above the sink. Inside the cage, with sunlight spilling in on it from the window, sat a green parakeet.

The little bird cocked its head and regarded her seriously.

Irena laughed and clapped her hands. "Hello, little one. Do you have a name?"

The bird squawked at her and shifted sideways along its wooden perch.

Irena came closer. "What a pretty thing you are. Don't be afraid."

The parakeet twittered and hopped about in the cage. It was so pretty, the feathers had such a lovely shading of green—light on the little chest, darker on the wings and the back. Irena had an overwhelming desire to touch it.

She unhooked the cage door and reached in. At once the bird began flapping its wings, beating against the wire cage.

"Calm down, little bird," Irena said. "I'm not going to hurt you. I only want to play with you a little, that's all."

She touched the downy chest feathers, and the bird hopped frantically to the far side of the cage. Laughing, Irena followed it with her hand. She stroked a finger lightly down its back. The delicate wings quivered under her touch.

Irena tickled its feet. The bird gave a high-pitched, frightened peep and beat its wings, flying hard against the top of the cage. With no way out, the parakeet seemed to give up. It dropped to the bottom of the cage with a soft *plop*. The tiny body shivered for a moment, then lay still.

Irena's laughter died. She cupped the small creature in her hand and brought it out of the cage.

"What's the matter, little bird? I didn't mean to hurt you. It wasn't my fault."

There was no movement from the tiny bundle of feathers. The bright little eyes were closed. The parakeet was dead.

Irena bit her lip. What a terrible thing to happen on her first day in Oliver's house. What would he think of her? The first thought that came to her mind was that she must replace the bird. She knew it would not be the same, but at least it would show Oliver how sorry she was about it.

She carried the dead bird back to her bedroom. On a shelf in a closet there she found a shoe box with crumpled tissue paper inside. She wrapped the parakeet carefully in the tissue, put it in the box, and replaced the cover. Then she hurried downstairs to find the Yellow Pages.

The shop Irena selected was called Bird World. It was located on a quiet street a block from Canal. For a minute she stood outside, getting her breath under control, then walked into the store.

A bell on a spring jingled over the door as she entered. For a moment there was utter silence, then the shop was filled with the twitterings of hundreds of birds. They were locked in cages along both side walls and in the rear of the store. Several parrots and cockatoos, and one macaw, were on freestanding perches, secured by little tethers on their legs.

A tall storklike woman approached Irena. "May I help you?"

The chitter of the birds grew louder. The macaw spread his wings in a threatening manner.

Irena set the shoe box down on the counter and took off the lid. Carefully she folded back the tissue paper, exposing the dead parakeet.

"Oh, the poor little thing," said the stork lady. "What happened?"

"I don't know. It just . . . died. I wonder if you have another one here like it?"

The woman prodded the dead bird with her finger. She turned it over. "I would think so. This isn't a rare species. Come along and I'll show you what we have in parakeets."

The woman started for the rear of the store. Irena came around the counter to follow her.

Immediately the birds set up a fluttering and flapping that sounded like a huge wind through loose branches. Their chirping grew shrill and urgent.

"I don't know what's got into them," the stork woman said.

As Irena followed her between the cage-lined walls, she felt surrounded by flapping, beating, screeching life. It was as though the birds were trying to break out of their cages to attack her. Or possibly they were trying to get away.

The woman stopped when they were just halfway back in the shop and turned to Irena. "I'm sorry. I don't understand what's the matter with the birds. I've never seen them act like this."

Irena looked sharply at the woman. Was there an

accusation in her tone of voice? Could she somehow know how the little bird died?

All around her the birds cried, "Killer!" A thousand bright little eyes glittered in panic. Cages clattered and banged as the birds threw themself heedlessly against the wire.

"I am sorry, but I'm going to have to ask you to leave," the woman said. "Something has badly upset the birds, and I'll have to close the store until I can get them settled down."

"Yes, of course." Irena took a last look around her, fighting down a growing panic of her own. She left the woman standing amid her terrified birds and fled, scooping the shoe box from the counter as she ran out.

Chapter 20

Billie Haines wandered unhappily among the grave markers in the New Orleans cemetery and thought black thoughts about the rotten vacation she was having after working for it all year in a Seattle insurance office. Like so many dumb mistakes, this had seemed like a good idea at the time. She thought she had it made when Carol Tetley suggested they share expenses on a vacation in New Orleans. Carol was the person Billie Haines would be if she could be reborn. Carol had naturally wavy hair, a perfect complexion, huge brown bedroom eyes, and tits that could stop traffic. The office studs hung around her like flies around a jam pot.

Not that Billie was such a dog. Actually, she was rather nice-looking. She simply did not have that secret ingredient Carol had that snapped men to attention. When she agreed to the joint vacation it was Billie's hope that some of Carol's magic might rub off. She fantasized about the platoons of dark-eyed men of New Orleans who, drawn to the gregarious Carol, would discover with pleasure the more subtle charms of her blonde friend.

Things had not worked out that way. Things had not even come close. They had arrived this morning, checked into a hotel, and gone into a local bar together this afternoon. Carol had attracted the men, all right, but as usual, Billie might as well have been invisible. She had sat with a smile frozen on her face, listening to the schlocky lines the men threw at Carol, praying that one of them might throw a little her way. None did.

Twenty minutes after they walked into the bar, Carol walked out with a bond salesman from Baltimore who looked like Burt Reynolds.

"You don't mind, do you, Billie?"

"Of course not." Oh, hell no.

"I'll see you later back at the hotel, okay?"

"Sure." Thanks heaps.

So here she was, wandering through a lousy cemetery trying to figure out how to kill the rest of the day. So deep in self-pity was Billie Haines that she did not see the approach of the tall man with the arresting eyes.

"It's quiet here, isn't it?"

She almost jumped out of her skin when the man spoke to her. Then she saw how good-looking he was and caught herself grinning like an idiot. Seemingly unable to stop herself, she babbled away about how she was not here for any morbid reason, and normally did not go strolling through graveyards, and she liked a little fun and excitement as well as the next person. One thing led smoothly to another, and even sooner than she had hoped Billie was having a drink with the tall stranger in a softly lighted bar.

"Paul is a nice name," Billie said, immediately regretting the inane comment.

The tall men did not seem to notice. His great luminous eyes watched her intently as she sipped the pink rum drink known locally as a hurricane.

"It's crowded in here, don't you think?"

Actually, Billie did not think so, but she was not about to disagree. "Yes," she said. "Lots of tourists, I guess."

"Can we go somewhere to be alone?"

It was like living out one of her fantasies. Trying to sound calm, she said, "My hotel isn't far from here. The room doesn't have much of a view, but—"

The man was obviously not interested in the view from Billie's room. Before she had the sentence out of her mouth he was signaling for the check, and a minute later they were leaving the bar, he with an intimate grip on her arm.

An hour after that both were in Billie's bed in the Hotel Emile Zola, naked. But Billie's romantic fantasy had come to a limp end some minutes before. Paul sat on the edge of the bed, his hands clasped between his knees, staring morosely at the floor. Billie reclined beside him, stroking his bare back.

"Don't be upset, Paul," she told him. "These things happen sometimes."

Without looking at her, Paul said, "You're a nice girl, Billie. I like you."

"Well, that's no problem," she said. "I like you too."

"You don't understand."

Billie squirmed around on the bed and rubbed her hand across his flat stomach, down to his groin. It was remarkable, she thought, how little hair he had on his body. And his skin was so smooth. Like a baby's.

"You're just a little nervous," she said. "Lie back. Relax."

Paul sighed. A deep sigh brought up from his soul. He let Billie ease him down on the bed.

"Every time I pray it won't happen," he said. "God knows I don't want to—"

"Hush now," Billie said. "It's not the end of the world. You just lie there and let Billie do the work for a change."

He lay back flat on the bed, staring at the ceiling as Billie kissed his chest, his stomach. Her hot little tongue explored his navel.

Billie felt the tension grow in his muscles as her lips brushed the silky hairs at his groin. She cupped his testicles in her hand, squeezing them gently.

Paul moaned. His flaccid penis stirred. He started to sit up.

Billie pushed him back down. "There, there, love, you just let me take care of this."

He lay back again, his arms straight at his sides, hands balled into fists.

Billie stroked the shaft of his penis. It grew. She kissed the head.

"There, you see?" she said, her lips touching the velvety flesh. She opened her mouth and took him inside.

Paul tried to protest as Billie's lips closed over him, but the words would not come. The warm, wet inner mouth sucked at him, caressed him, brought him rapidly toward the release he so badly craved. And feared. It was too late now to stop it. He raised his hands to his face, saw the fingers bent into claws.

His back was pressing on something cold. There was a bright light shining in his face beyond his closed eyelids. He heard the splash of running water.

Paul opened his eyes. It took a moment for him to get oriented. He was lying naked on the tile of a bathroom floor. Water was running from the faucet into the sink above him. He looked at himself. His bare skin was moist and paler than ever.

It had happened again.

He got shakily to his feet and stood before the bathroom mirror with both hands braced on the sink. He turned off the blasting cold water and leaned closer to the glass to study his reflection. His pale, smooth flesh was unmarked, except for a flap of grayish membrane that adhered to his stomach. He peeled it off as one would peel a sunburn, raised it to his mouth and ate it.

He dreaded opening the bathroom door, but there was no postponing it. He had to go out through the bedroom. He wiped his face on one of the hotel towels and went out.

It was as bad as he feared. Blood was everywhere—in soggy pools on the carpet, spattered on the walls, even a streak of dark red on the ceiling. The rumpled bed sheets were soaked crimson. Tangled up in the bloody bedclothes were bits and pieces of the woman who had been Billie Haines, insurance secretary from Seattle.

Paul stepped carefully over the blood-soaked patches of carpet to the chair where his clothes lay neatly folded. On the floor near his shoes was a hand. It had been severed well above the wrist. Broken bones and gristly tendons protruded from the raw end. The hand lay palm up, the fingers reaching out as though in supplication.

He put on his clothes quickly, being careful not to look at the hand. When he was dressed, he eased open the door and peered out into the hall. For the moment it was deserted. He slipped out of Billie's room, letting the door latch behind him. He walked swiftly past the elevators, heading for the stairway.

Chapter 21

Oliver was tired when he keyed open the door to his little house on Burgundy Street. Riding around for hours in a vibrating helicopter, looking for the elusive black leopard, had left him with an aching back and a throbbing head. The thought of spending a relaxed evening at home with Irena cheered him.

He walked into the house. There were no lights on downstairs, and the room was in deep shadow.

"Irena?"

"Over here, Oliver."

He jumped at the sound of her voice. As his eyes adjusted to the gloom he saw her sitting at his writing table, hands folded in her lap. He walked over to her.

"Are you all right?" He looked closer and saw the redness of her eyes. "You've been crying."

"A terrible thing happened today," she said.

"What?" Visions of monstrous attacks on the girl flashed through his tired mind.

There was a shoe box on the writing table. Irena pulled it over between them and gently unwrapped the tissue paper inside. Oliver looked in at the tiny body of the parakeet, then back at Irena.

"It's Peppy."

"I'm so sorry, Oliver."

He took the girl's hands and pulled her up so she stood facing him. "Darling, Peppy was just a bird. Birds die. He was getting old for a parakeet, anyway."

"He didn't just die, Oliver. I killed him."

"What do you mean?"

"I was only playing with him. I didn't want to hurt

the little thing. I just reached into the cage to touch him and . . . and he fell over. He was dead."

"You couldn't help that," Oliver said.

"No, listen to me, I think I frightened him to death."

"That's foolish, Irena. I told you Peppy was an old bird. It isn't your fault in any way." He put his arms around her, but she did not respond. Looking over her shoulder he saw for the first time her suitcase sitting on the floor next to the table.

"What's that?"

"It's better that I leave here, Oliver."

"Don't talk crazy. It was only a bird."

"That's not all of it. This afternoon I went downtown to a store where they sell birds. I was going to buy you a new one. But when I walked into the store all the birds started acting strangely. The closer I came to them, the more frantic they were. There's something wrong with me, Oliver. Those birds were terrified of me."

"Be reasonable, Irena. There could be any number of explanations for what happened."

"It's in the blood. That's what Paul told me. My mother and father, the way they died, now my brother. It's a taint that could be in my blood too. I don't want to involve you."

"Stop it," Oliver said. "There is no reason for you to believe that whatever has happened to Paul has anything to do with you."

"I think it does," she said quietly. "It will be better for both of us if I leave."

"You can't!" Oliver blurted. Then more calmly he added, "You can't leave, because I love you."

The tears Irena had been holding back spilled over and rolled down her cheeks. She hugged him. "Oliver, oh, Oliver, how can you love me when you know what I am? What I might become?"

160

"Hush, darling. This has been a rough couple of days for you."

"It's not just what's been happening, it's what can happen in the future."

"Did you hear me say I love you?"

"Y—yes."

"I didn't mean just for tonight. What I mean is there will be two of us standing together in the future. You won't have to fight alone."

Irena looked up into his face. There was a hunger in her eyes. "Oh, I want so much to believe it can be that way."

"It can, darling," he said. "It can be any way we want to make it."

He kissed her, and this time she responded with her whole body. But after a minute she pulled away again.

"What if I told you I can't go to bed with you? Would you still want me to stay?"

"There's no rush about that. I want everything to be right for us."

"No, Oliver, I mean what if I could *never* make love to you the way I want to?"

"We'll talk about it," he promised, "but not tonight. We're both too tired to make heavy decisions. Let me take your bag back up to your room."

Irena did not object as he carried her suitcase up the stairs to her bedroom. They kissed lightly as she stood in the doorway, then Oliver left her and went to his own bed. He lay there for a long time running their conversation over in his mind, trying to understand what it meant.

Shortly after dawn he was awakened by the insistent ringing of the telephone. He stumbled down the stairs and grabbed the instrument, still not fully awake.

"Yeah?"

"Oliver? This is George Brant."

"Who?"

"Detective Sergeant George Brant, New Orleans Police Department."

"Oh, yeah. What's the matter?"

"I'd like you to come down to the Hotel Emile Zola. There's been a killing here."

"Somebody I know?"

"A tourist. Her name was Billie Haines."

Oliver was rapidly waking up and getting irritable. "The name means nothing to me. What's the matter, Sergeant, don't you have enough detectives?"

"This looks like the work of your leopard."

"In a hotel?"

"Don't ask me how or why, but that's what it looks like. The Haines woman was literally torn to pieces in her room. I've seen a lot of murder victims, but I've never seen one ripped apart like this. No human being could do it."

"All right," Oliver said, "I'll be there as soon as I can."

He hung up and stood for a moment frowning down at the telephone. What the hell kind of a cat was this? Massage parlor? Hotel? He picked up the phone again and called Alice Moore.

"Can you be ready to go downtown in ten minutes?" he said when her sleepy voice came on the wire.

"I guess so. What's happening?"

"You wouldn't believe it over the phone. I'll fill you in on the way downtown."

He loped back up the stairs and met Irena standing in the hall outside her room.

"What is it?" she asked.

"There's been . . . some new evidence of the leopard. They want me to check it out."

Irena started to turn back toward her door. "I'll get dressed and go with you."

"I don't think that's a good idea," Oliver said. "You stay here, and I'll get back as soon as I can."

Irena's eyes narrowed. "Didn't you just call Alice?"

"That's right. Alice is a professional, and she can be helpful to me."

"And I'd just be in the way."

"Please, Irena, this is just something that I have to handle."

"You and Alice."

"Well . . . yes, damn it."

Irena turned and walked into her room. She closed the door firmly behind her. Oliver started to follow, then thought, to hell with it, and continued to his own room to get dressed.

The Hotel Emile Zola was not one of the Old World establishments with wrought-iron balconies that are found throughout the French Quarter. Neither was it one of the gleaming new high-rises along Canal Street. Built in the 1950s, it was a conservative-looking place that catered to families and tour groups. It offered a minimum of frills at reasonable prices, all within easy walking distance of the Quarter.

The lobby was in a turmoil when Oliver and Alice walked in. Policemen were arguing with a loud news crew from a local television station, members of the hotel staff were apologizing to the guests, and everybody was talking at once.

Sergeant Brant bulled his way through the confusion to Oliver and Alice. He led them past the police guard into an elevator.

Brant punched the button for the third floor. "I'm not sure the lady ought to see this," he said.

"If you mean me," Alice said, "I didn't come all the way down here to go fetch coffee."

The detective rolled his eyes.

"Alice will be all right," Oliver assured him.

"Whatever you say."

The third-floor hallway was filled with policemen who were directing unofficial traffic away from room 312. Brant pushed open the door and stood aside so the newcomers could see.

Alice gasped. Oliver felt a lump of bile rise in his throat. The detective watched their reaction with a certain grim satisfaction.

"You tell me," he said, "could a man have done something like this?"

Oliver swallowed hard. "They say Jack the Ripper left them pretty bloody sometimes."

"But he used a knife. Like I told you on the phone, this woman was ripped apart."

"Didn't anybody hear anything?" Oliver asked.

"Oh, sure. Neighbors in the next room heard what sounded like animal growls. Also some screams. Trouble is, they didn't think about reporting it until after the body was found."

"Why on earth not?" Alice asked.

"They thought it was part of a tour group from South America having some fun. Didn't want to get involved."

"Wonderful," Oliver said drily.

"Nobody remembers seeing the victim come in last night. Her roommate was out on some party of her own. She came tiptoeing in about 4 A.M., and this is what she found.

Oliver knelt to examine a disembodied hand that lay on the blood-soaked carpet. The marks on the ragged flesh were almost certainly teeth.

"It does look like an animal attack," he said. "A particularly vicious one."

"There's something else I want to show you," Sergeant Brant said.

He beckoned Oliver over to the bed. "Walk around

the outside edge of the carpet. There's no blood out there." When Oliver joined him he pointed to the wall above the headboard of the bed. "Our friend might as well have left his signature."

There on the pale yellow wallpaper was the huge bloody imprint of a paw.

"What about it?" Brant asked.

Oliver examined the print. "It's a big cat, all right. Most likely a leopard."

"Is it ours?"

Oliver closed his eyes. The hours with the veterinarian reports and his own repeated measurements left no room for doubt.

"Yes," he said. "It's our cat."

Chapter 22

The sun, just risen in the eastern sky, made a glittery path across Lake Pontchartrain as Oliver turned the pickup off Interstate 10. He drove on an unpaved road through the marshy woodlands that lay along the western shore of the lake. In the back of the truck were fishing gear and overnight provisions. Beside him on the seat, Irena was silent and thoughtful.

"Believe me," Oliver said, "it's best that you didn't go with me yesterday. The way that hotel room looked will give me nightmares for a month."

"Will it give Alice nightmares?"

He looked at her quickly, caught the mischievous smile, and grinned in return.

"It will do us both good to get away from the city for a day," he said. "And from that damned leopard."

"It *is* pleasant out here," Irena agreed.

"Don't expect too much of the jetty house, now. A tough old fisherman, Yeatman Brewer, and I put it up practically with our bare hands. The roof leaks, and it's too cold in the wintertime, but this time of year it's kind of fun."

"Does your friend live there?"

"Yeatman? No, he has a place of his own a couple of miles up the lake. He takes care of the jetty house and uses it when he has a fishing party to take out. I just come out once in a while when the pressure of the city gets me down. Spend a day or two. Fish, cook outdoors, swim . . ."

"Have you brought other women out here?"

166

Oliver turned to look at her, but her expression was innocent.

"I've had parties."

"With Alice?"

"Alice has been out here, yes." Oliver pulled to a stop at the lake shore, anxious to get off the subject of Alice Moore. He helped Irena out of the truck and pointed at a rough wooden cottage that sat out on the end of a jetty. "There it is."

"It looks cozy," Irena said.

"Better than a hole in the ground, as Yeatman would probably say."

They walked out on the jetty as the choppy waves of Lake Pontchartrain lapped at the pilings beneath their feet. A rangy, grizzled man in a rough woolen shirt stood in the doorway of the house.

"Hey, Oliver," the man said, "I got the shack all opened up and aired out for you. Had a bitch of a time gettin' rid of the fish smell."

Oliver shook his hand. "How you been, Yeatman?"

"Holdin' my own, you might say. How 'bout yourself? Looks like you're doin' right well, if this little gal is any sample."

"Irena, this is my friend Yeatman Brewer."

She shook the fisherman's hand. "I've been hearing about you."

"Nothin' good, I'll wager," he said, cackling.

They went into the house, while Yeatman stayed in the doorway. Oliver stood off to one side while Irena turned slowly around in the center of the room. There were Coleman lamps, a few pieces of sturdy furniture, a big window overlooking the lake. The walls were decorated with Oliver's animal photographs.

"I like it," she said, turning to include both Oliver and Yeatman in her smile. "I really do."

"It has a certain rustic charm," Oliver said, pleased.

167

Irena walked over to where a beaded curtain closed off a corner of the room. She rattled the beads aside, revealing a low full-sized bed.

"Parties, hey?" she said to Oliver with a glint of mischief in her eyes.

Oliver coughed into his fist. "I'll go out to the truck and get the fishing gear. The earlier we get out, the better they'll be biting."

"You gonna be needin' me for anything else?" Yeatman asked.

"No thanks," Oliver told him. "We can handle it from here."

"Kinda thought you could," the old fisherman said. "I'll come back to clean up tomorrow night." He gave them a broad wink and sauntered out the door.

Oliver and Irena spent the next thirty minutes loading the stubby rowboat Yeatman had left behind, then Oliver rowed them well out into the lake, where they began to fish.

He was happy to see the girlish enthusiasm Irena showed when she pulled in a black bass or a sunfish. Her eyes glittered with pleasure as she yanked the flopping creatures from the water, expertly unhooked them, and tossed them into the catch bucket. There was no sign of the moodiness that had come over her in recent days.

They lunched in the boat on sandwiches packed the night before in New Orleans. Oliver drank beer from a six-pack of Budweiser he'd brought along. Irena had her usual carton of milk.

When they had all the fish they could eat, it was still early, so they just let the boat drift while they talked and laughed and enjoyed each other's company.

About midafternoon they took their catch back to the jetty house, where Irena insisted that Oliver show her how to clean the fish. She proved remarkably deft with the gutting knife, and showed none of the usual female revulsion at scooping out the innards.

In the evening they went ashore. Oliver built a big campfire and they fried the fish in sizzling fat in an iron skillet with only salt and pepper for seasoning. Oliver could not remember a more delicious dinner in his life. Irena ate with the same hearty appetite he had admired the night they met.

When the fish were eaten, the fire drowned, and the cooking gear rinsed and stowed in Oliver's pack, they started back toward the jetty, their arms linked.

Irena stopped suddenly, holding him back.

"What is it?" he said.

"Listen," she said softly.

Oliver peered at her in the gathering darkness. "Listen to what?"

"The sounds of the night. The little creatures all around us talking to each other."

Oliver held his breath and tried to concentrate on the chirping and chittering of small animals in the woods, but all he could think about was taking this beautiful girl into his arms. So that is what he did. And he kissed her.

Irena kissed him back eagerly. Her mouth opened. Her tongue met his. Oliver's hand slipped inside her blouse, touched her breast.

Abruptly she pulled away from him. "Oh, God, I'm sorry. That was my fault."

Oliver groaned. He ached with the wanting of her.

She moved close again and touched his cheek with cool fingers. "I know, darling I want it too."

"Then why—?"

"It isn't our time," she said. "I have to be . . . sure about something."

"How sure can you be?"

She looked up at him with sad, dark eyes.

He breathed deeply several times, filling his lungs with the cool air off the lake. "Okay. You take the bed tonight. I'll get out the trusty sleeping bag."

"Please bear with me, darling," she said. "I promise you I'll have things sorted out in my head soon."

He smiled and touched her hair as it ruffled in the light breeze. "Soon," he repeated.

The day spent out in the fresh air, the exercise of rowing, and the satisfying fish dinner combined to put Oliver into a deep sleep ten minutes after he stretched out on the floor in the sleeping bag. Not so Irena. She had never slept well at night, preferring to nap during the daylight hours. On this night she found it even harder to sleep than usual. The sound of Oliver's regular breathing, the lapping of the wavelets against the jetty, the creaks and groans of the pilings, all seemed unnaturally loud.

And there were other sounds. The voices of the night creatures that she had heard so clearly when they were leaving the campfire. The voices floated to her now across the water. She could almost make out what they were saying.

After a wakeful hour she peeled back the sheet and blanket and stepped out of bed. Carefully she drew the beaded curtain aside and went into the room where Oliver lay in the sleeping bag. It was dark, but Irena had no trouble seeing. She walked across the floor without making a sound and crouched beside Oliver. She looked down into his face, and one of her hands stole inside her nightgown and felt her breast where he had touched her. She squeezed it gently, wanting Oliver's hand there. Releasing her breast, she slid the hand down across her stomach to her groin. She massaged herself, eyes closed, yielding to a momentary fantasy.

Her own breathing grew more rapid. Quickly she

stood up, crossed the room, and slipped out the front door into the darkness.

The night sounds were much louder outside. Irena inhaled, breathing in the night like a perfume. Moving with unconscious grace, she walked the length of the jetty and started through a field of ankle-high grass to the woods. She kicked off the light slippers, which she found suddenly uncomfortable, and continued barefoot into the woods.

The trees closed in around her like a group of welcoming friends. The breeze off the lake fluffed her hair and cooled the fever of her cheeks.

The sounds around her intensified. As they did so, the shadows of the forest lightened and gave up their secrets. Irena found she could see into every corner and crevice.

A mouse scampered through the grass with a great crashing noise. A thunderous flapping overhead turned out to be the flight of an owl. A methodical crunching, grinding was the insect life in a rotted tree stump. She heard a high, almost feminine scream as the swooping owl seized the mouse in its talons. A panicky hum from behind her was a fly caught in the web of a spider. An ominous twang sounded as the spider hurried along a silken strand to claim its prey.

Irena was part of it all. This was where she belonged. She stood in the center of a small clearing and let the life of the night seep into her. She turned slowly, tasting it.

There was a movement in the grass, and a rabbit hopped into view. It stopped, nose twitching, looking this way and that, alert for predators. Irena looked at the rabbit and smiled. The rabbit saw her. Its sudden rapid breathing was like the whimper of a frightened child. It darted away. Irena sprang after it.

*　　*　　*

Oliver was awakened by a sudden cool breeze on his face. The closing of the door to the outside snapped him fully awake.

He could see nothing in the darkness. With muscles tensed, he listened. There was the soft pad of footsteps across the planks of the floor. A dark silhouette came toward him.

"Irena?"

He sat up and fumbled for the flashlight, thumbed it on. In the instant that the light shone he saw her standing hunched before him, her eyes wild, blood on her mouth and streaking the front of her nightgown.

"Don't look at me!" she cried, and kicked the flashlight out of his hand.

Chapter 23

It didn't really happen.

Irena stared into the mirror over her dressing table and repeated the words to her reflection.

Back here in Oliver's cozy house on Burgundy Street it was not hard to believe that the whole terrible night had been some wild imagining. The house on the jetty, the beckoning woods, the night voices, the rabbit, the blood . . . None of it seemed real when viewed from this safe distance.

And yet it *was* real.

Irena was too sensible a young woman to live in a world of pretense. It had all happened, just the way she remembered it. Oliver had been very good about it the next morning. After politely asking her if she was all right, he said nothing at all about her appearance the night before. By that time Irena had cleansed her face and her body, and had stuffed the bloody nightgown deep into her bag. As calmly as she could, she had told Oliver that she felt fine.

Thinking about Oliver now brought a lump to her throat. He was the kindest, most gentle, and understanding man she had ever known. More than that, he stirred up passions within her that Irena hadn't known were there. That was where the danger lay for both of them.

She looked down from the mirror to her sketchbook and continued with the drawing she had worked on throughout the early morning.

A soft rap at the door.

Oliver's voice: "Irena, are you awake?"

"Just barely," she answered. "I'm not dressed."

"I have to go out now," he said. "I should be home about six."

"I—I'll be here."

A pause, then, "I love you."

Irena caught her lip between her teeth. Her eyes misted. There was silence for a moment while Oliver waited for her reply, then the sound of his footsteps going down the stairs.

Irena pulled a Kleenex from a box on the table and wiped her eyes. She balled it up and threw it away, forcing herself to concentrate on the drawing in her book. It was her own face, but with small, grotesque changes. The eyes were more slanted, staring intently out from the page. The nose was broader, the mouth shaped differently, the ears tapered back. It was as though she were in the midst of some ghastly metamorphosis.

Impulsively Irena slashed back and forth across the drawing with the soft pencil, scarring it with crisscross lines until the lead snapped. Then she put her head down on her arms and cried bitterly.

"We're calling off the search," said Detective Sergeant Brant.

Oliver, sitting at his desk in the zoo administration building, while Alice Moore stood behind him, frowned.

"It's been five days since the woman was killed in the hotel room," Brant continued, "and no sign of the cat anywhere in the city since."

Oliver tapped the end of a pencil on his desk. "Somehow I feel he's still out there."

"I don't see how. A black panther that size—"

"Leopard," Oliver corrected automatically.

"Right, leopard. Anyway, a cat that size can't wander around a city of half a million people for almost a week without somebody seeing it. The thing can't turn invisible. I say he's either dead or he's left the state."

"A dead black leopard is just as visible as a live one," Oliver pointed out. "I can't believe we're rid of him that easily."

"There's nothing I can do about it," the detective said. "We don't have the manpower to devote any more time to cat hunting."

"Yeah, the budget," Oliver said bleakly. "I know how that goes."

"What about Paul Gallier?" Alice asked.

"Him we're still looking for," Brant said.

"Any leads?" said Oliver.

"Not yet, but we'll get him. And when we do, he should be able to answer a lot of questions for us."

"I hope so," Oliver said, but his voice held no conviction.

The detective said his goodbyes and left the office. Alice walked to the window and stared out. Oliver watched her, feeling uncomfortable.

"I think we ought to talk," she said.

He waited.

"About us."

"All right."

Off in the distance thunder grumbled. The curtains at the window stirred uneasily.

"Storm on the way," Oliver said.

"Things haven't been the same between you and me since Irena came," Alice said.

"It's been . . . difficult," Oliver said evasively.

"Are you in love with her?"

Oliver squirmed under the direct questioning. "I don't know, Alice. There's something about Irena. Something I can't define."

"Have you gone to bed with her?"

175

"No. I feel kind of, well, protective."

"Protective?" Alice repeated. "That girl doesn't need your protection. What she needs is professional help. There's something not right about her."

"That's not fair," he said.

"I'm not trying to be fair. I'm trying to find out where things stand with you and me."

Oliver glanced uneasily at the open office door. "We can't talk here."

"Then let's go somewhere tonight where we *can* talk."

"I don't want to leave Irena alone."

"Then let's go to your place," Alice said. "We've got to have this out, Oliver, and Irena probably ought to be in on it, anyway."

Oliver sighed heavily. "All right. You and I will go to my place, and we'll all talk, if that's what you want. I'm not convinced it's the right time, though."

The rain started at four-thirty in the afternoon. The sky was a deep slate gray, and lights were turned on all over the city.

In her room upstairs in Oliver's house, Irena napped, curled on the bed. A sudden gust of wind blew a spray of rain in through the open window and across her face. She got up and padded across the room to close the window. As she started to turn away a flash of lightning lit the scene outside in stark relief. Irena froze. Crouched in the branches of the tree outside her window was her brother, Paul.

Irena started to back away, but before she had gone two steps Paul sprang from his perch. The window glass exploded inward and Paul dived into the room, landing gracefully on all fours. A lamp was knocked off the dressing table. It lay on its side on the floor and threw distorted shadows across the wall.

Outside the storm gained in fury, whipping the curtains into the room. Thunder crashed like cymbals, and rain drummed on the roof.

Paul Gallier bounced to his feet and moved lightly around Irena. He placed himself between her and the door.

"Hello, little sister."

"Paul, what's happened to you?"

"Many things, most of them bad. You are the only one who can help me now."

"The police are looking for you."

"I know." His eyes pinned her. "Set me free, Irena."

"I don't know what you mean."

"Yes, you do." His voice rose dangerously. "You've got to help me."

"I can't do anything for you, Paul. You're not well."

"You're just like me, Irena. In your heart you know it. By freeing me, you will free your own true spirit. We will make each other free in the same way our father and mother did. They were more to each other than man and wife, you know. They were like us."

"No!" Irena held her hands over her ears. "I won't listen to you. You're lying."

Paul grasped her wrists and pulled her hands down. "It's you who are lying, little sister. Lying to yourself. You think you love this Oliver. You tell yourself you can live a normal life with him. That is the lie, and you know it. All you can bring to your Oliver is death. Come with me, little sister. Join with me so we can both be free and live as we were meant to."

A blinding flash of lightning was followed immediately by the boom of thunder.

"Oliver loves me," Irena said.

"No, he doesn't. He loves the cat. He loves the animal, because he fears it and wants to possess it. He would possess you too, if he could, but you cannot

177

belong to any man. Let your Oliver go to the redheaded woman. They belong together. Your place is with me, little sister. Come close and let me show you."

"No!" Irena wrenched her hands free and backed away from him.

Paul's expression darkened. He dipped suddenly and picked up a dagger-shaped splinter of window glass and came toward her.

"If you will not join me, then we must both die." His eyes were wild as he advanced.

Irena backed away from him until her shoulders hit the wall. Paul moved in quickly. He brought up the shard of glass and pricked her throat. Irena felt the blood trickle down.

"Don't, Paul. Don't do it."

"There is no other way," he said. "This will end the agony for both of us."

She saw that he was completely irrational now. It was no good trying to reason with him.

"All right, Paul," she said, making her voice soft and caressing. "I'll do whatever you want. I'll come with you." She put her arms around him. Paul pressed his body against hers.

Irena kissed him tenderly—his eyes, his cheeks, his mouth. There was a soft clink as the dagger of glass fell from his hand to the carpet.

Paul's hands massaged her back, and they sank slowly together to a kneeling position. He continued to move lower, kissing her breasts through the thin material of her blouse. He stretched out prone, kissing her stomach. He mashed his face into her groin.

Hot little stabs of pleasure shot through Irena's body. This was wrong, it was sinfully wrong, but she wanted him to do it. Using all the strength of her will, she reached out and picked up the pointed fragment of glass from where it had fallen. She raised it over Paul's head as he continued to nuzzle her. The back of his neck was exposed and vulnerable. One slash and it would be all over. She told herself to strike, but she hesitated for another second.

In that second some animal sense warned Paul. He raised his head and saw the dagger of glass at the instant Irena started to bring it down. He threw up a hand to ward off the blow. The glass sliced through the tender flesh on the inner part of his forearm.

Blood spurted. Paul cried out in pain and surprise. Irena slashed at him again, but he spun out of her reach.

Using the momentary respite, Irena leaped to her feet and ran to the door. Across the room Paul gripped his wounded arm and stared at her. She snatched the key from the inside of the door, slammed the door, and locked it from the outside. Out in the hallway she leaned against the wall, fighting to get her breath. There was no sound from the other side of the door.

Inside the room Paul stared down at the blood flowing from the long, clean cut on his arm. He held the wound to his mouth and sucked on it. The blood ran down his chin, spattering his clothing.

Across the room he saw himself reflected in Irena's mirror. The shape of his eyes had changed. They were slanting now, the irises yellow, the pupils narrowed to vertical slits.

Paul opened his mouth, salty with his own blood, and growled softly. The flesh on his fingers began to split and peel away.

Chapter 24

The wind-driven rain washed across the windshield of the pickup truck like a blast from a fire hose. Oliver could safely drive no faster than twenty miles an hour. His knuckles were bloodless as he gripped the steering wheel. Beside him Alice Moore sat leaning tensely forward, trying to peer through the sheet of water that spilled across the glass.

When at last he pulled up at the little house on Burgundy Street, they both leaned back for a moment to let the tension drain away. Then they looked at each other, nodded, and made a dash for the front door.

When they were inside the house Oliver snapped on the lights. They stood dripping rain water in the entranceway.

"I could use a cup of coffee," Oliver said.

"Want me to make it?" Alice offered.

"Thanks. I'll go get some towels."

Alice started for the kitchen. Oliver climbed the stairs and went to the linen closet at the end of the hall. He selected a couple of big bath towels and was starting back toward the stairs when he noticed the seam of light showing under the door to Irena's room. He walked over and rapped lightly.

"Irena? How about a cup of coffee? Alice is downstairs."

There was a shuffling sound from inside the room, but no answering voice. For the first time Oliver saw the key in the outside of the door.

"Irena? Are you all right?"

The crack of light at the bottom of the door blinked out. From inside the room came a crunch that sounded like someone walking over broken glass. Oliver turned the key, pushed open the door, and went in.

"Irena?" Sudden fear was a cold knot in his belly. Quickly he crossed the room to the broken window. Cold rain lashed him in the face.

The door slammed behind him. A key turned.

Oliver whirled. In the darkness of the room he thought he saw something vaguely human crouching in the corner. It growled at him.

Lightning forked into the ground not far away, and the room was floodlit a brilliant white for a fraction of a second.

Paul Gallier hunched naked against the far wall. Or some ghastly parody of Paul Gallier. His lips were drawn back to reveal cruel pointed teeth. The eyes had an inhuman yellow glow. The skin of his face and body was badly wrinkled, and seemed to be peeling away.

The room was plunged back into darkness. Oliver stared hard at the shadowy shape crouching against the far wall. He tried to speak, but found his throat had tightened on him.

"Oliiiver-r-r . . ." It began as a semblance of human speech, but ended as the rumbling growl of an animal.

Oliver backed away as the thing that had been Paul Gallier crawled toward him across the glass-littered floor. Its breath came in heavy snorting pants as the thing came nearer.

Lightning blazed again. Any resemblance the thing in the room may have had to Paul Gallier was gone. Six feet away, glaring at Oliver with a jungle hatred, was the black leopard. Its sudden roar was a thundering bellow in the small room.

"Oliver?" Alice's voice called faintly from downstairs. "What's up there?"

Oliver had no time to answer. He backed along the

wall, searching frantically for something to use as a weapon against the advancing cat.

The leopard, belly to the floor, slid forward a measured step at a time. A bass growl rumbled in its throat. The heavy black tail switched from side to side, thumping the carpet like a club.

"Oliver?" Alice was closer now, on the stairs.

"The gun, Alice!" he shouted. "Get the rifle out of the bookcase!"

The leopard raised one huge paw. A solid blow from that, Oliver knew, could break his leg. Or his back. His foot bumped against something metallic. He reached down and found the fallen gooseneck lamp. Oliver snatched it up like a drowning man going for a log. It was not much of a weapon for fighting off a man-killing jungle beast, but it was better than his bare hands. He only had to hold the animal off until Alice got back with the rifle. *Only!*

The leopard sprang at him. Gripping the flexible neck of the lamp near the shade, Oliver swung the heavy metal base down like a hammer. He caught the leopard on top of the broad skull, surprising it more than he hurt it. With the momentum of its spring gone, the cat retreated a step.

When she heard Oliver's shout, Alice sprinted back down the stairs two and three steps at a time. At the bottom she found the glassed-in bookcase where Oliver had stowed the bolt-action Winchester from the zoo. She seized the handles of the glass doors and jerked on them. Locked.

In a growing panic, she looked around for something she could use to break the glass. She picked up a heavy elephant figurine and threw it at the bookcase, flinching away as the glass shattered. She reached inside, careful to avoid glass splinters, and pulled out the rifle.

182

Holding the gun before her, she started running back up the stairs, then stopped suddenly.

My God, is it loaded?

Alice levered the bolt back and stared into an empty chamber.

Oh, Goddamn! Where would he keep the ammunition?

Alice tried not to listen to the sounds coming from upstairs as she ran back down to the bookcase.

Please let the bullets be there!

She used the butt of the rifle to knock out the bits of glass that remained in the door frame, and stared inside. There, lying loose on the bottom where Oliver had put them when he unloaded the Winchester, were five steel-jacketed cartridges. Breathing a prayer of thanks, Alice scooped them up and shoved them one at a time into the breech.

Upstairs Oliver continued to do what he could to hold the leopard at bay with the gooseneck lamp. After he connected with the first blow to the head, the cat advanced more warily. As he came within reach, Oliver swung again, aiming for the leopard's tender nose. This time he was not fast enough. With a sudden slash of his paw the leopard hooked the base of the lamp and tore it from Oliver's grasp. It flew through the air and clanked against the far wall.

With no weapon left to him, Oliver scrambled away. The cat, as though wanting to prolong this moment of triumph, came slowly, deliberately after him.

Turning to the bed, Oliver snatched up the blanket and wrapped it around his forearm. When the leopard came for him he raised the padded arm in defense. There was a flash of claws and the blanket was reduced to ribbons.

"Alice!" Oliver cried. Why the devil was she taking so long?

Moving frantically along the walls while the cat padded after him, Oliver overturned any piece of furniture he could move, trying to put obstacles between himself and the beast. The big cat swatted them aside like cardboard toys.

While keeping his attention riveted on the leopard, Oliver could not look where he was going. Inevitably, he found himself backed into a corner. There was nowhere he could go where the leopard could not reach out and gut him. As a last desperate measure he jerked the mattress from the bed Irena had used and held it out before him as a shield.

When the leopard hit it, it felt to Oliver as though a car going at full speed had slammed into the mattress. Amid the snarling and ripping sounds the cottony mattress stuffing exploded into the bedroom. It floated gently around the man and the cat, settling on the carpet like a soft snowfall.

The claws raked Oliver's chest, his stomach. He looked down in horror at the angry red furrows in his flesh.

A sudden thumping at the door.

"For God's sake, Alice, shoot it open!"

The muscles of the cat rippled under the glistening black coat. It was tensing for the final assault. Oliver seized a pitifully fragile chair and held it out. The cat splintered it with one contemptuous blow.

The talons ripped Oliver's shoulder and down his arm. His vision began to blur as the pain paralyzed him.

An explosion out in the hallway, and the door burst inward. For one frozen second the leopard and the wounded man stared at the woman standing in the doorway with the rifle to her shoulder. The cat turned and started toward her. Alice fired.

The leopard bounced into the air, spun around, and hit the floor awkwardly.

She fired again. The impact of the second bullet knocked the cat off its feet. It struggled to a sitting position and twisted its head back, trying to bite at the wound in its side. Then, with a baleful look at Alice, the animal dragged itself toward the window, and had its front paws on the sill when Alice fired the third time. This one blew the big cat out through the broken window. The heard the body land with a soggy thud on the rain-soaked ground below.

Alice dropped the rifle and pushed her way through the debris to where Oliver knelt in the corner of the room. Blood covered his face and soaked through the front of his shirt. He opened his eyes and gazed blankly at Alice for a moment. Then his face cleared.

"What took you so long?"

Impulsively Alice took him in her arms, paying no attention to the blood that stained her dress. They held each other for a moment, then stiffened as outside there rose a deep, wailing howl.

"That thing can't be alive," Alice said in a hoarse whisper. "I shot it three times. All solid hits."

The howling came again.

"Help me to the window," Oliver said.

Together they struggled to the broken window and stood there as the rain pelted in on them. Below, stretched out on the lawn, with its black face staring blindly into the rain, lay the leopard. Kneeling beside the dead cat, stroking its wet fur, was Irena. She raised her face to the night and howled.

Chapter 25

In death the black leopard looked even larger than it had when it was alive. It lay on a white enameled table under fluorescent lights in the laboratory of the zoo administration building. Oliver Yates, bandaged and pale, stood beside Sergeant Brant, looking down at the dead animal.

"Big sonofabitch," said the detective.

"Mm-hmm." Oliver was thoughtful.

"Beats the hell out of me where he's been hiding. Or how he found his way to your house."

"Coincidence, maybe," Oliver suggested.

"Coincidence, my ass. That sucker came looking for you. Or for the Gallier girl. Somehow, against all the laws of nature, he found you."

"There is still a lot we don't understand about animal behavior," Oliver told him.

"And I, for one, would just as soon leave it that way." The policeman switched his attention from the dead leopard to Oliver. "He ripped you up pretty good. Are you sure you're going to be all right?"

"Luckily, none of the wounds went really deep," Oliver said. "I promised to go back to the hospital and get the dressings changed when I'm through here. But first I want to get an autopsy done on this beast. Care to hang around and watch?"

"No, thanks. It's bad enough that I'm forced to watch them do these on humans. Anyway, my case isn't closed. I still have to find Paul Gallier."

"Well, good luck, George."

"Same to you." With a last look at the dead cat, Brant left the building.

From a tray of gleaming instruments, Oliver selected a heavy scalpel. He strained to roll the leopard's body so it lay belly up, then poised the scalpel for the first incision, starting right under the chin.

Gauging the depth of his cut so he would not damage any internal organs, Oliver slipped the blade into the dark flesh and sliced in a straight line down the length of the cat's belly. Satisfied that he had made a clean cut, he lay the scalpel aside and picked up a pair of forceps. He gripped the skin with the flat tips of the forceps and began to peel it back.

Immediately he recognized that there was more resistance than there should be. He lay the tongs aside and bent down for a closer look. There, just beneath the flap of hide he had peeled back, was a second layer of skin—pinkish, translucent . . . and human.

Oliver straightened up fast. "Jesus Christ," he muttered.

He began to strip away more of the animal hide. The two layers of skin were connected by gristly threads. He had to use a long-bladed scalpel, held sideways, to separate them.

Sweating heavily as he worked, Oliver finally had a large portion of the leopard's skin laid back from the belly and clamped. There inside the cat, distorted still by the animal skeleton, was the unmistakable form of an evolving human being. The head, tucked forward on the chest, bore the face of Paul Gallier.

Fighting down an impulse to gag, Oliver stepped back from the table. He watched in disbelief as the half-formed man within the leopard shuddered. An arm flopped out of the opened cat's belly and smacked wetly on the metal table top. The distorted head raised on the neck and began to wobble from side to side.

"Oh, God, no!" Oliver said. *"No!"* He realized he was shouting in the empty room, and clapped his mouth shut.

The grotesque pale thing inside the cat continued to shudder and flop about. Oliver took up the long-bladed scalpel and forced himself to approach the table again. Clamping his right wrist with his left hand to steady it, he drove the stainless steel blade into the pale flesh of the oversized embryo.

There was a sudden hiss and a gurgling sound. Oliver jumped back as a foul smelling yellow-brown liquid spurted from the carcass, splashing over the dissecting table and spilling onto the floor. As the noxious liquid bubbled out, the body of the leopard, and what was inside it, shrank and sizzled and twisted on the table until only a fleshy coil remained in a pool of mucus.

Oliver gave himself five minutes to sit down and pull his nerves together. Then he set to work cleaning up the mess.

In the New Orleans City Jail Irena Gallier sat in a hard wooden chair and faced Femolly through a mesh of heavy-gauge steel wire.

"My brother is dead," Irena said.

"I know that," said the tall black woman.

"How can you know?"

"I feel it." A single tear rolled from each eye down the coffee-colored cheeks. "You must not think of your brother as a bad man. He did not choose to be what he was."

"What *was* he, Femolly? What am I? What makes us the way we are?"

Femolly glanced over at the door. A jail matron stood there with her arms folded, bored, paying no attention to the conversation.

"A long, long time ago in another land there was a race of people who gave their children to the gods when they were angry. Those old gods were the giant cats. Little by little, over many lifetimes, the souls of the little children got all mixed up with the souls of the cats. One became the other. Both became one. Most of the race has vanished long ago, but a few live on today."

"And I . . . I am one of those people?" Irena said.

"Your father and your mother were. And their father and mother. And your brother. What do you think?"

"Is there nothing I can do? No place I can go?"

"Accept your fate, child. There is no changing it, and there is no hiding from it. You must go and seek your own kind."

"But there is a man . . ."

"Listen to Femolly. You can never be happy with people who are not like you. You can only bring destruction to them and to yourself. As your brother did."

"No!" Irena sprang to her feet, upsetting the chair.

The matron snapped out of her daydream and hurried over. "What's the trouble here?"

Irena ignored her. She said to Femolly, "I won't accept that. I can't live that way. It isn't fair. I want to love and laugh and find my happiness like other people. I have done nothing wrong."

Femolly spoke calmly. "What you are is not your fault, child, any more than the color of my face is mine. But you'd best accept it."

"Never!" Irena cried.

The matron stepped in and tried to quiet her, but Irena spun away and ran out of the room. When she was out of the building and into the sunlight she stood on the sidewalk breathing hard.

She had a *right* to be happy. Femolly had to be mistaken. Irena resolved that she would have her happiness. Nothing and nobody was going to stand in her way.

Chapter 26

mistaken ... nobody ... that she would have ... happiness. Nothing and nobody was going to stand her ...

Alice Moore pounded rhythmically along the asphalt jogging path that circled the park. She concentrated hard on the coordination of her arm and leg movements, her breathing, the rate of her heartbeat. She thought about how the asphalt felt under the soles of her Nike joggers, the shrill chirping of the birds, the look of the sky through the elm branches overhead, the sharp smell of fresh-cut grass. She focused her mind on anything except her relationship with Oliver Yates, and how it had started to come apart the day Irena Gallier walked into their lives.

Alice licked at her upper lip and tasted the salt of her perspiration. Good. If she got nicely tired, maybe she could sleep tonight without the tormenting visions of Oliver and Irena together.

She rounded the corner and the setting sun threw a long gangly shadow of a running woman on the path ahead of her. Alice frowned. The setting sun meant it would be getting dark soon. Not a good time for a woman to be out jogging alone. Not even through a well-kept park in an upper-middle-class neighborhood like this one. Rather than make the complete circuit of the jogging trail, she decided to cut across the park to St. Charles Avenue and catch the streetcar there for home.

She turned off the asphalt onto a narrower path of hard-packed dirt. The regular slap-slap of her shoes changed to a softer thud.

She had gone only a short distance when a chill seized her. Something had changed. What was it? Alice concentrated on her surroundings. The birds. Where were the birds? Their noisy chirping had been cut off as though by a knife. The only sound now on the darkening path through the park was the cushioned impact of her Nikes.

Alice jogged on, puzzled and worried. Had her presence on the path frightened the birds into silence? No, they had been chattering busily away just seconds before. What could it mean?

Before she could come up with an answer, there was an explosion of sound above her head. She looked up to see hundreds of birds flap into the air and wheel off and away.

Strange. Alice's feeling of something being wrong grew stronger. She tried to concentrate on maintaining the rate and rhythm of her jog, but small fears pulled at the corners of her awareness.

Something rustled up ahead where the brush was thick and filled with shadows. A low overhanging branch moved, shaking suddenly for no visible reason.

Leopard! The thought hit her like a fist in the stomach.

No, she reminded herself angrily. The leopard was dead. She had personally killed it. Oliver had cut it open this morning on a dissecting table at the zoo. It must have been an unsettling experience, because he flatly refused to talk about it.

The branch quivered again.

The wind. No, there was no wind. With a sudden increase in her pulse rate, Alice ran on.

The cat flew out of the tree black as death and screeching like a banshee. Alice stumbled and almost fell. She opened her mouth to scream, then held it in. The little black house cat, tail fluffed in alarm, landed on the path in front of her and scampered off through the brush.

Boy, have I got a case of nerves, Alice thought. She laughed in relief. The presence of the little cat would account for the strange behavior of the birds too. She picked up the pace again and jogged on.

The sun was almost down. Only the tops of the elm trees caught its fading light. Along the path where Alice jogged, the shadows merged into a pervading gloom. Her relief at seeing the little cat drained away, and the anxiety came back. The feeling of being watched. Of something following her.

She stopped at a water fountain, drank a little, gargled, and spat the water out on the ground. She wet her fingers and flicked droplets on her face and neck.

What was that?

A twig snapped. Something was moving in the brush.

Shape up, girl, Alice told herself. It was probably the little kitty cat still hanging around. She had to get her nerves in shape.

But it was dark now. The lights along the path were dim and spaced far apart. Time to get the hell out and get home.

Alice started along the path again, holding an easy pace to prove to herself that she was not panicky. Just jog along nice and steady, think about your body, and before you know it you'll be out of the woods and onto friendly, familiar St. Charles Avenue.

But damn it, there *was* something behind her. She could distinctly hear padded footfalls other than her own. Running. And not two feet, but four.

Without consciously willing it, Alice speeded up. The running feet behind her speeded up too. Whatever was back there was gaining.

Alice was on the verge of breaking into an uncontrolled run. Through her mind raced bloody pictures of slashing teeth and ripping claws. She saw again the torn-apart body of the woman in the hotel room. Her breath was coming in ragged gasps. Perspiration soaked her jogging suit.

"How many miles?"

Alice almost fell at the sound of the male voice close behind her. She forced herself back into a coordinated pace as two men wearing shorts and sweat shirts jogged up beside her. White, middle-aged, friendly looking. Obviously not muggers or rapists. And definitely not a black leopard.

"I'm sorry," Alice got out, "what did you say?"

"How many miles you go?" the man repeated. He was wearing glasses. Smiling.

"I—I don't know. I don't keep track."

The second jogger, blond and soft around the middle, spoke up. "We try to do twenty a week. Heaven knows, I could probably use more."

Alice managed a weak smile.

The runner with glasses said, "St. Phillip's is sponsoring a 10-K run next month. I don't know if you're into that, Miss . . . uh . . ."

"Alice Moore."

"Hi. I'm Father Harn," said the first jogger.

"And I'm Father Jessup," said his blond companion.

Priests. Jesus Christ, they were priests. "Happy to meet you," Alice said. She laughed. "I am *really* happy to meet you."

The two priests jogged along beside her. They looked at each other in mild puzzlement.

The clank of a passing streetcar sounded like a heavenly chorus to Alice. When the path turned to parallel the avenue, she slowed.

"This is where I leave you," she said to the jogging priests. "Good night."

"Good night," said Father Jessup. "It's been nice talking to you."

"Don't forget the 10-K run," said Father Harn.

"I won't," Alice said. She pulled off the path and stopped for a moment to watch the two men jog out of sight. Then she cut across the avenue to a streetcar stop.

She jogged easily in place to cool down as she waited for the trolley. There was no one else waiting at the stop. In fact, St. Charles was uncommonly deserted tonight.

No, there was someone coming toward her along the sidewalk. A woman. Alice stood in a pool of light from a streetlamp. The other woman was in shadow, and she could not see the face.

The woman stopped abruptly. She stood twenty yards away in the darkness and stared at Alice. Something about the woman brought back all the fears of Alice's jog through the park.

At a hissing shriek behind her, Alice's heart jumped into her throat. She whirled, hands out in front of her defensively, only to see the pneumatic doors of the streetcar folding open. Weak with relief, she boarded the car.

She dropped her fare into the box and found a seat by the window, halfway back in the car. As it started to move, she peered out through the glass at the dark sidewalk. The woman was standing there still, her face hidden by the shadows, watching.

By the time she entered her apartment building, Alice had convinced herself that her nervousness in the park and on the street was entirely due to an overactive imagination. A vigorous swim in the pool was just what she needed to soak the tension out of her muscles and calm her frazzled nerves. She passed by the elevators and took the stairs down to the gym.

The gym instructor hired by the apartment association was a sturdily built girl named Sandra. She was just coming out of the gym as Alice approached.

"Do I have time for a swim?" Alice said.

"I was just closing up."

"All I want is a quick dip. Just enough to stretch the muscles. Be a pal, Sandy."

"Well . . . five minutes, okay?"

"Wonderful."

Sandra selected a key and handed it to Alice. "No more than five minutes, now."

"Promise."

Alice unlocked the door to the pool area and went in. The water glowed blue and inviting, illuminated by lights below the surface. Alice flipped the wall switch and the big overhead fluorescents went on. She felt a little nervous at being the only one in the cavernous room.

At a bench along the wall she sat and pulled off the Nikes and sweat socks, then peeled off her jogging suit. Wearing only bikini panties, she ran across the tile deck and dived in.

The pleasant shock as Alice's body cleaved the cool water revived her spirits. She glided along close to the bottom, letting the momentum of her dive carry her half the length of the pool. She planed upward and broke through the surface, blowing and splashing like a happy seal. She went into a crawl and did two strenuous laps, then breast-stroked another. She rolled on her back and floated for a minute, then eased into a languorous backstroke, trying to do it as gracefully as Esther Williams in those old movies.

A metallic *clack* echoed off the concrete walls. Alice broke off in mid-stroke and rolled her head to look toward the door. No one there. She resumed the backstroke, watching the overhead lights glide slowly by.

Without warning the lights went off.

Alice rolled over, swallowing some water. She coughed, keeping herself afloat in the middle of the pool, and looked again toward the door. This time she saw a shadow that moved over by the light switch.

"Hey, what's the idea?" Alice called. "My five minutes isn't up yet."

There was no answer, but suddenly the underwater lights went dark. For a moment Alice felt utterly abandoned, floating in a limitless black void. The water was cold and unpleasant against her flesh.

"Sandy?" she called, knowing in her heart that it was not Sandy who had come in and killed the lights.

Gradually her eyes accustomed themselves to the gloom. The only light came from the glowing EXIT sign over the door. It was sufficient for Alice to see the shadow that moved low to the floor along the edge of the pool

"What do you want?" she said, not expecting an answer. She continued to tread water, keeping well away from the edge of the pool where she had seen the moving shadow. Her ears were attuned for the smallest sound, her eyes straining to pierce the near-darkness.

Something growled.

In sudden terror Alice lashed out toward the ladder at the deep end. When she reached it, the menacing shadow was waiting at the top. She paddled back, trying to keep the shadow in her vision.

A loud creak just above her head startled her. She looked up and saw the diving board dip. Something was edging out on the board.

In full panic now, Alice thrashed toward the other end of the pool. Her feet scraped against the bottom. She stood up and began to wade clumsily toward the steps leading up out of the shallow end. The shadow thing was there again, waiting for her.

Splashing wildly, Alice clawed her way back to the

center of the pool. She was tiring fast. Her arms ached. A knot was forming in her stomach.

She pulled in a lungful of air and screamed for help. The sound of her voice echoed in the cavernous pool room. She screamed again.

All the lights came on.

"Alice, is that you?"

Shading her eyes against the sudden dazzle of lights, Alice peered in the direction of the voice.

"Are you all right?"

Standing by the light switch just inside the door was Irena Gallier.

"What are you doing here?" Alice demanded. She coughed some pool water out of her windpipe. "Why have you been following me?"

"Following you?" Irena came over and stood at the edge of the pool. "I don't understand."

"Like hell you don't."

The door opened. Both women turned to look as Sandra came in.

"What's going on?" the instructor said.

Feeling ridiculous as she tread water out in the pool, Alice pointed at Irena and said, "She . . . she followed me in here. She turned out the lights and was trying to . . . get at me."

Irena looked hurt. "Alice, I don't know what you're talking about. I didn't find Oliver at the hospital, and I thought he might be here. I came looking for him. I'm awfully sorry if I frightened you."

Alice stared at her. The girl seemed so sincere, so innocent. Was it possible she was imagining all these crazy things?

Sandra stood with her hands planted on her hips, looking suspiciously from one of the women to the other.

"I'll say good night, then," Irena told them with a

friendly nod. She turned and walked out through the door.

"What was that all about?" Sandra asked.

"Oh . . . nothing," Alice said, realizing the impossibility of explaining her fears.

"Are you about finished in here?"

"I'm finished," Alice said. "I'll bring the key out to you."

Sandra went out, letting the door hiss closed behind her. Alice walked up the steps and out of the water at the shallow end, shivering out of control. She hurried across the cold tile to the bench where she had left her clothes. She picked up the jogging suit and began to shake violently. The shiny green suit had been sliced to ribbons.

Chapter 27

Oliver sat slumped on the sofa in his living room. Lying on the cushions on both sides of him and in his lap were photographs. There were pictures of the black leopard live and the leopard dead. There were snapshots taken of Irena the day they went fishing at the jetty house. He had spent hours going over the pictures, examining them in minute detail, comparing them, searching for . . . *what?*

What the hell *was* he looking for? Oliver asked himself for perhaps the twentieth time this evening. He picked up the sheet of drawing paper that was the most troubling picture of all—Irena's self-portrait from her sketchbook. The catlike alterations in her face were terrifying to him, but the thing had no meaning.

It seemed nothing made sense any more. The memory of what he found when he cut into the leopard's corpse still haunted him. Had he made a mistake by not telling anyone? But who would he tell? With no evidence, who would believe him? Would he believe a wild story like that if he heard it from somebody else? Not bloody likely.

He looked at all the pictures again. The leopard, Irena, Irena with the face of the cat. What the hell did it mean? Oliver lay his head back against the sofa cushions and closed his eyes. He was more tired than he realized, and in less than a minute he was asleep.

His dream was a mixed-up thing of giant cats and naked women with blood on their mouths. From somewhere a high-pitched voice called to him, trying to tell him something urgent. The voice called to him over and over and . . . became the ringing of the telephone.

Oliver jumped up, spilling the photographs onto the floor, and stumbled across the room to the telephone. He grabbed up the receiver.

"Hello?"

Before he could get the word out there was a click and the hum of a dial tone. Damn, why couldn't they have hung on another five seconds? Now he would worry the rest of the evening about who was trying to call him. As though he didn't have enough to worry about already.

In her apartment Alice drummed her fingers on the telephone after hanging up in frustration. Where could Oliver be? She felt it was urgent that she tell him about the bizarre events of the evening—her sense of being followed in the park, the silent woman who watched her get on the streetcar, the menacing shadow at the pool, Irena's strange appearance, and the destruction of her clothes. Alice was sure that Oliver was in danger. She was the only one who could warn him. She would try his number again in a few minutes in case he had stepped out only briefly.

Oliver started to return to the photographs, but thought better of it and headed for the stairs. A good night's sleep would help him straighten out his thinking. He had intended to sit up until Irena came home from wherever she had gone, but there was no point in that if he was just going to fall asleep on the sofa.

He went into the bathroom upstairs and carefully removed his shirt to have a look at the wounds left by the leopard's attack. Nothing had soaked through the dressings, that was good. He peeled back the bandages and saw that the scratches were healing nicely. He washed them out and daubed on medication from a tube. As he capped the tube he heard the telephone ringing again. He started for the stairs, but before he got there the ringing ceased. Puzzled, he walked back to the bathroom.

Alice chewed on a thumbnail as she listened to the burr of the telephone ringing in Oliver's house.

"Please be home," she muttered. "Please answer the phone."

There was the sound of somebody picking up at the other end. Alice went weak with relief.

"Oliver, where have you been? I've been trying to reach you. Something happened tonight that you'd better know—"

A click on the other end, and the line went dead.

Alice stared at the instrument in her hand as though it had bitten her. He couldn't have hung up. Rapidly she dialed Oliver's number again. This time she heard the maddening buzz-buzz of the busy signal.

Damn! What was going on? She jammed the button down, held it there for several seconds, and dialed again. Again the busy signal. Weeping with frustration, she slammed the receiver back into the cradle. The recent storm must have screwed up the lines. Alice pounded the tabletop with her fists.

In the dark living room of Oliver's house the telephone receiver lay on the table next to the cradle. The dial tone hummed faintly, but no one listened.

Upstairs Oliver pulled on a light terry-cloth robe, belting it carefully so as not to irritate his wounds. Where was Irena? he wondered. Then he grinned crookedly at his image in the mirror. He was acting like a worried father. However, his feelings for Irena were anything but fatherly. Besides, it was only a little after nine o'clock. He decided to go downstairs and find a book to read until he fell asleep.

In the living room he stopped halfway to the row of books on the mantel. A cold breeze was coming in from somewhere. He looked around and saw the window open over his writing table. When he walked across to close the window, he saw the telephone lying off the hook.

What the hell was going on here?

Oliver replaced the telephone receiver, then lowered the window. As he did so he was startled to see the reflection of Irena in the dark glass. He spun around to face her, and for a long moment they stood without speaking. She had a strange look. Wild.

The telephone rang. Again. On the third ring Irena picked up the receiver and handed it to Oliver without saying anything.

Alice's voice came filtering through the earpiece. "Oliver? Is that you?"

"Yes."

"You sound funny. Are you all right?"

As Alice spoke to him, Irena walked over to the standing lamp by the front door and snapped it out.

"I'm all right," Oliver said. His eyes followed Irena. "What is it, Alice?"

"I called you before. I don't think your phone is working right."

Irena crossed the room and turned out a second lamp, leaving only one soft light in the room.

"It's working now," Oliver said distractedly.

Slowly, her eyes never leaving him, Irena began to undo the buttons of her blouse.

"It's Irena," Alice said over the phone. "She followed me tonight, Oliver. There's something wrong with her. Something dangerous. Oliver? Do you hear me?"

Irena slipped the blouse back off her shoulders and

let it fall to the floor. She wore no brassiere. Her pale breasts were firm and high. They seemed to glow in the soft light.

"I hear you," Oliver said into the mouthpiece.

Irena opened the single button at the side of her skirt and slid the zipper down. Oliver's mouth was dry as he watched her push the skirt down her slim legs. She stood up, wearing only a pair of lacy panties, and looked at him with a challenging smile.

"She may come to your place," Alice continued. "Maybe you should get out of the house."

Irena's body was slim and smoothly muscled. She ran her hands down over her breasts, across her stomach. Oliver swallowed hard.

"I'll be all right," he said.

"Do you want me to come over there?" Alice asked.

Slowly Irena turned away and walked toward the stairs. She moved with a liquid grace.

"No, I think it's best that you stay where you are," Oliver said into the phone.

Irena started up the stairs.

"Are you sure?"

"I'm sure. Look, I'll call you back, Alice."

He hung up the phone and looked toward the stairway, where Irena had disappeared. Then he went after her.

She was lying in his bed, covered by a single sheet. The lacy panties lay on the floor. Irena smiled up at him, an impossible combination of innocence and depravity. She turned down the sheet beside her, inviting him. One pale breast was exposed, the dark nipple like an eye watching him.

Oliver stood for a moment at the foot of the bed, not moving.

"What's the matter?" she said. "Are you afraid of me?"

He hesitated, then said, "Yes, I think I am."

She threw off the rest of the sheet and lay naked before him. "Don't be afraid, my Oliver. I want us to belong to each other."

He unbelted the robe and shrugged it to the floor. Underneath he wore only the bottoms of his pajamas. He pushed them down and stood before her as she ran her eyes over his body.

Irena propped herself up on one elbow. Gently she touched his scars with the tips of her fingers.

"My poor Oliver. Does it hurt much?"

"Not much," he said.

"Come down here with me."

He sat on the edge of the bed. Irena raised herself to a sitting position beside him. He lightly touched her hair, her face, her lips.

"Are you sure this is what you want?" he said.

"Yes. This is our time, Oliver."

He kissed her. Her bare arms went around his back and pressed him close against her. Irena's mouth opened hungrily and she took his tongue.

Oliver kissed her chin, the hollow of her throat. She lay back on the bed. His lips moved to her breast. She moaned as he sucked at her nipple. She pushed it firmly into his mouth. The resilience of her flesh against his teeth aroused him ferociously.

He moved his head down the center of her body, tasting the sweet-salt of her flat stomach, the fluff of her pubic hair. Irena squirmed on the bed, her fingers locked behind his head. Oliver nuzzled her soft mons, kissed the warmth between her legs. He tasted her, probing with his tongue.

Suddenly Irena sat up. She drew Oliver's face up to hers and kissed his mouth, still wet from her body's juices. Her hand strayed down his body, found his erect penis, stroked him.

She pulled back her head and looked him in the eye. There was a wildness about her that Oliver found agonizingly desirable.

"Now," she said in a hoarse whisper. "There is no going back for us."

She guided him gently over on his back, then knelt above him, her legs straddling his body. She bent down and kissed him, licking his face. Bit by bit she lowered herself upon him. She touched his erection, then took him inside of her a centimeter at a time. She began to ride up and down, slowly at first, then more vigorously. She cried out softly as the barrier gave way, then abandoned herself to the lovemaking.

They clung to each other, lunging and walloping on the bed, breathing hard through open mouths. Finally the climax burst upon them, and they laughed aloud with the sheer joy of fulfullment.

They subsided slowly and at last lay quietly in each other's arms. For a long time they stayed like that, not wanting to break the contact made by their bodies. Irena was the first to pull away.

She sat up in the bed. "Look at me, Oliver."

He raised himself on his elbows and smiled at her.

"What do you see?"

"I see a beautiful, sensual, very loving woman."

"There's nothing . . . different about me?"

"Your hair's messed up."

"I'm serious. There is nothing . . . strange?"

"Absolutely," he said.

She began to cry, but there was a little smile on her lips. "I was so afraid . . ."

Oliver pulled her back down beside him. "There was nothing to be afraid of."

"I thought something might happen."

"Something did," he said softly.

"I mean . . . something terrible."

"Mmmm." Oliver's voice trailed off, his eyes closed, and he slept.

Irena smiled down at him tenderly. In a little while she disengaged herself from his arms and eased out of bed, being careful not to wake him. She went into the bathroom, turned on the light, and stood back from the mirror to examine herself.

Everything seemed to be as it should be. She touched her skin. It was smooth and warm. And firm. She felt the dampness between her legs and put her hand down there. Her fingers came up bloody.

The sight of her own blood on her hand frightened her at first, then fascinated her. She turned on the water tap in the sink and held her fingers in the stream. The pinkish water swirled around the bowl and down the drain.

She got into the shower then and adjusted the water temperature as hot as she could stand. She soaped her body thoroughly and rubbed herself with a rough washcloth. Then she soaped all over again and rinsed. Finally she turned the water all the way to cold and forced herself to stand under the needle spray until her teeth chattered.

She stepped out of the shower, toweled herself pink, and again examined her body in the mirror. Nothing there but a naked young woman who had just been very well taken care of by the man she loved. Irena smiled in vast relief.

Before leaving the bathroom Irena brushed her teeth, working up a minty foam in her mouth, rinsing, and spitting into the sink. She cut off the water and wondered at the deep bubbling sound that continued after all the water had run down the drain. When she left the bathroom she could still hear it—a kind of liquid throbbing that left her vaguely troubled.

She returned to the bedroom, where Oliver still slept

peacefully. The boiling sound was still in her ears, now with a growing drumlike beat.

Did all women hear this secret sound after they made love? Irena wondered. Or was it only the first time? She crawled into bed beside the sleeping Oliver and pulled the covers up to her chin.

The rumbling sound continued. It grew louder. Somehow Irena was reminded of the woods out by the jetty house. She saw also another, denser forest. One where she had never been. Irena began to fear that the bubbling rumble would wake Oliver.

Her hands began to itch.

She brought her hands out from under the covers and held them before her eyes. Something strange was happening to them.

Irena sat up in bed, her back braced against the headboard, staring at her hands. The skin on her fingers and palms began to wither and crack. Her fingers shrank back and grew thicker. The fingernails loosened and dropped out like dead flower petals. Thick, curved talons broke through the flesh beneath them.

Her mouth fell open in a grimace of pain and shock. Her gums burned as her teeth, bloody at the roots, loosened and fell out, pushed by the fangs coming up from below.

She tried to speak, but managed only a moaning howl.

Oliver awoke with a start. He sat up and turned at once to Irena, who was sitting on the edge of the bed, facing away from him. She was hunched over, shudders wracking her body.

He reached out to touch her but snatched his hand back. Beneath her skin he had felt the vertebrae shifting and snapping.

"My God, what's happening?" he cried.

Slowly, with things still squirming under her skin,

Irena turned to face him. Oliver stared in naked horror at the fangs that protruded from her mouth. Her cheeks caved in and her nose began to widen. It was the face she had drawn in her sketchbook.

Irena screamed. The voice was no longer human. She reached for her eyes with clubby, clawed hands, and as Oliver watched, horrified, pulled them out.

Behind the pulpy balls of her human eyes glowed the amber eyes of the leopard. They blinked at Oliver as he scrambled away, trying to disentangle himself from the bedclothes.

One of Irena's disfigured hands grabbed his arm, the talons pinning him where he was. He was forced to watch as the woman's flesh began to split, first on the forehead, then over her entire body. It made a soft tearing sound.

As the pink human skin peeled away, the dark form inside struggled to free itself. The head shook vigorously back and forth, ripping free of the damp membrane that had enclosed it. The thing emerged black, and glistening wet as a newborn baby. It tore with its teeth at the fleshy covering, pulling it away, chewing it up, swallowing it. In minutes there was only a thick pinkish pool of residue where the woman Irena had been. In her place was the cat.

The leopard threw back its head and rejoiced in the triumph of its freedom. The roar thundered through the house.

Left alone for a moment, Oliver started to edge off the bed. The leopard struck faster than the eye could follow, slamming a heavy black paw down on either side of him, pinning him flat on the bed. The terrible black face moved down close to his own. He could feel the fur of the cat's belly against his bare skin.

Oliver's heart hammered in uncontrolled fear. The cat's breath was a blast of heat in his face. He rolled his head from side to side, searching vainly for some way to escape.

The leopard raised one massive paw and put it down flat on his chest. Oliver watched the claws slide out of their sheaths and prick his flesh.

"Irena!" he cried, the breath blasted from his lungs.

The cat lifted the heavy paw. Oliver sucked in air as the leopard began to lick him. The rasplike tongue tore away the scabs and lacerated the flesh.

Oliver tensed, waited for the powerful jaws to crush his bones. The leopard raised its head and looked into his eyes with an almost casual curiosity. Oliver turned his head away, and the cat imitated his movement.

Then, playfully, the leopard butted his chin with its broad forehead. The blows were solid, and they hurt.

"Don't," Oliver said. He raised a hand tentatively to the face of the cat. Before he could pull it back, the jaws clamped down on his wrist. He could feel the knife-sharp teeth against his flesh, but the leopard did not bite down. It gave his arm a couple of gentle tugs, then released him. The fangs left little dents, but had not broken the skin.

My God, Oliver thought, the thing is playing with me.

He was beyond panic now, just numb. He felt almost detached as the cat opened its great mouth and took most of his head inside. Oliver lay paralyzed. He felt the rush of the cat's hot breath, the roughness of its tongue, the hard points of its teeth. Abruptly the beast pulled back and looked at him again, its head cocked to one side.

"Damn it, let me go!" Oliver shouted, surprised at the sudden strength of his anger.

The leopard growled and raised one massive paw, claws bared. Oliver braced for the stunning blow he expected. The paw shot out toward his face. Two, three, half a dozen times it struck before he could blink. The pillow beneath his head was shredded, the sheet that covered him destroyed, the mattress deeply ripped on both sides of where he lay. As the attack ended, Oliver opened his eyes to find himself miraculously untouched.

The bed shook as the leopard leaped from it to the floor. At the window the beast turned back to look at him. In that instant Oliver saw the soul of the woman reflected deep in the amber eyes of the cat.

"Wait!" he cried, but the cat turned from him and, in a single graceful bound, glided out through the window.

Oliver heard the rush of leaves as the leopard landed in the tree outside. Then a thump as it dropped to the turf below, and padded footfalls dwindling into the night.

"Be careful," he said to the darkness. "Oh, my darling, be careful."

Chapter 28

When Alice Moore arrived at Oliver's house, a city police car was standing at the curb. Its flashing red light threw an intermittent glow onto the trees out in front. She hurried to the front door, found it open, and went in without bothering to knock.

Oliver was sitting on the couch. He was wearing khaki pants and an open shirt that revealed the angry scars on his chest from the leopard's claws. Standing in front of him was Detective Sergeant Brant. Both men turned to look at Alice as she entered.

"Irena has been here, hasn't she," Alice said. It was not a question.

Oliver nodded. He was having trouble meeting her eyes.

"We've got more serious things to worry about than that," said Brant.

Alice raised her eyebrows.

"Unbelievable as it may seem," Brant continued, "we've got another black leopard on the loose."

"You're sure that's what it is?" Oliver said.

"Not a doubt in the world. We've got it hemmed in now on the causeway. I thought you might like to be there at the finish."

Oliver got painfully to his feet. "Yes, I definitely would. Could you drive the truck, Alice? I'm a little stiff."

"Sure, if you want me to." Alice glanced at the bookcase, where the rifle had been replaced behind the broken glass doors. "Are you going to take that?"

Oliver hesitated, then he said, "I suppose I'd better."

He picked up the rifle and walked out with Alice. Sergeant Brant got into the police car and took off to lead the way.

In a few minutes they arrived at the south end of the twenty-three-mile causeway across the center of Lake Pontchartrain. The near end was blocked off by a row of police vehicles just beyond the tollbooths. Their massed headlights were trained out onto the bridge, and brought the scene into bright relief. Half a mile out into the lake another row of headlights stretched across the road. Halfway between was the black leopard. It prowled from side to side on the causeway, peering first in one direction, then the other. Oliver felt a catch in his throat as he recognized the helplessness of the trapped creature.

"There it is," said Brant. "We seem to be having a regular epidemic of those babies."

Oliver turned to look at the row of flak-jacketed policemen who stood beside the flanked vehicles. They carried heavy weapons and held them at the ready.

"What do you expect the cat to do," Oliver said, "charge you with a machine gun?"

"Listen, after all the static we took about letting the last one get away, we're not about to take any chances on losing this one," Brant said.

"Couldn't we try to capture it?" Oliver suggested.

"Not this time," Brant said with finality. "The mayor isn't going to accept anything other than one dead leopard." He turned to a policeman who lay on top of one of the cars with a scope-sighted rifle. "Ready, Art?"

"Whenever you say, Sergeant."

"No!" Oliver said suddenly. He pushed his way past Sergeant Brant and started walking out along the causeway.

"Hold your fire!" Brant shouted to the man on the

car. Then to Oliver, "Where the hell are you going? Come back here!"

Oliver ignored him and continued to walk. He shaded his eyes against the dazzle of the headlights at the far end.

The leopard stood motionless, watching him come. Its eyes were yellow jewels in the bulky black shadow.

Behind him a bullhorn crackled. Sergeant Brant's voice boomed through the night. "Oliver, come back here. Leave the leopard where it is. We can't protect you at this range."

Oliver walked on.

When he came to within a few feet of the cat, it tossed its head and loosed a thunderous roar. Oliver froze, waiting for the cat to make the next move. Effortlessly it sprang to the rail at the edge of the causeway.

"It's going over!" somebody shouted.

"Don't let it get away!"

There was the crack of a rifle, and a bullet sang off the rail near the spot where the cat stood balanced. Another shot came from the ranks of the policemen. Then quickly another, and another.

Oliver dropped to his stomach as the fusillade grew heavier. Bullets raised sparks where they hit, and their whining filled the night. The leopard stood poised on the rail for a moment longer, then dived gracefully into the dark water.

Oliver jumped up and ran to the rail. Several yards from the causeway he saw the head of the black leopard, ears laid back, as the animal swam powerfully toward the southwest shore. There was another burst of gunfire, pocking the surface of the lake all around the head of the swimming cat. Oliver cringed, imagining the impact of the bullets on his own body.

Suddenly the head of the cat disappeared beneath

214

the dark water. The gunfire dwindled and stopped. Searchlights played over the surface, but there was no sign of the animal.

Alice and Sergeant Brant ran out to join Oliver at the edge of the causeway.

"Did they get her?" Alice asked.

Sergeant Brant looked at her curiously. "Her?"

"I don't know," Oliver said. "The cat went under and didn't come up again."

"As far as I'm concerned, it's a dead leopard," Brant said. "It's more than a mile to shore from here, and I don't think there's a cat in the world can swim that far. Especially if we put a couple of bullet holes in it. What about it, Oliver?"

"You're probably right for any ordinary cat," Oliver said.

Alice and Sergeant Brant looked at him questioningly, but Oliver was staring out over the dark, unbroken surface of the lake.

To Alice he said, "Would you mind riding back to town with the sergeant?"

"I suppose not, but—"

"Thanks. There's something I have to do. I'll call you as soon as I get home."

While Alice and Brant gaped after him, Oliver jogged back along the causeway past the row of police cars. He hoisted himself painfully into the truck, swung it around to face in the other direction, and roared off into the night.

Chapter 29

Oliver pushed the truck to its limits. He wheeled along the southern shore of Lake Pontchartrain and turned off on the smaller road leading into the marshlands to the west. The road came to an end and he jammed to a stop. Seizing the rifle from the space behind the seats, he jumped out of the cab and ran toward the jetty.

He took a shortcut through the edge of the woods, but found that the low-hanging branches slowed him down. He had to keep one arm up in front of his face to fend them off.

When he was almost out of the trees he pushed one hanging limb out of the way, then snatched his hand back. He looked more closely and saw it was a human arm. Up in the tree, his body jammed head-down into a V of branches, was Yeatman Brewer.

Oliver jumped back, all his senses alert now, and looked around. Nothing moved. The little night creatures were unnaturally still. Laying the rifle aside, he wrestled Yeatman's body down out of the tree and eased it to the ground. The ragged rips in Yeatman's throat and chest told Oliver clearly how he had died.

"I'm sorry, old friend," he said softly.

Picking up the rifle again, Oliver moved on, more cautiously than before. When he reached the jetty he stopped and peered out at the dark bulk of the house he and Yeatman had built. There seemed to be a faint light inside, but no movement that he could see.

He waited until his breathing returned to normal, then gripped the rifle in one hand and ran out the jetty toward the house. He kept his body low, making as little noise as possible.

He stopped when he came to the house, and leaned against the wall for a moment. The door stood open. Inside he could see the glow of a Coleman lamp turned very low.

Oliver stepped warily through the door. A floorboard creaked under his weight. He froze for ten seconds, with the rifle held ready to fire. The faint glow of the lamp was coming from behind the beaded curtain that closed off the bed. Oliver crossed the room in swift strides, reached out, and swept the curtain aside.

Irena was sitting on the edge of the bed. She wore an old pair of his jeans and a T-shirt that he kept in the jetty house. Her hair was damp. She looked up at him calmly.

"I knew you would find me," she said.

"You killed Yeatman," Oliver said.

"Yes. I'm sorry."

"He died in my place, didn't he?"

"Yes."

"Why him, Irena? Why not me?"

"Because I love you," she said. Her eyes filled with tears.

"God help me, I love you too," Oliver said.

"Do you really?"

"Yes, Irena. Really."

Her eyes moved down to the rifle in his hand. "Then use that. Kill me."

He did not move.

"It's the only way, Oliver. You know what I am."

He nodded.

"Then you know that I must die. You saw what I did to your friend. I will do that and worse to others. To Alice, maybe."

Sweat broke out under Oliver's arms and rolled down his sides. He shivered with a chill.

"Do it fast, Oliver. I want you to be the one."

He raised the rifle and levered a cartridge into the chamber. Irena turned her face away. He looked down the barrel at her through the sights.

Slowly he lowered the rifle.

"I can't do it."

"Please. You must."

"No. There has to be another way."

Irena stood up and faced him. "There *is* one other way."

"Yes?"

"Free me. Make love to me one more time. Then I will leave you forever and seek out others of my own kind."

Oliver shook his head. "I can't."

"You can!" Irena stripped the T-shirt off over her head. She took his hand and held it to her breast.

To his astonishment, Oliver felt himself becoming aroused.

"I know you can," Irena purred. She unzipped the jeans and skinned them down her legs. She stood up naked and came into his arms.

Oliver let the rifle slip to the floor and held her. Her skin was still cool from the lake water, but it warmed quickly to his touch. He kissed her. Irena's tongue probed deeply into his mouth. She tasted like wild blackberries.

Irena stepped back from him. "Do you have some rope?"

"Why?"

"I want you to tie me to the bed. That way I can't hurt you when I . . . change."

"But afterward . . .?"

"Afterward you will leave me. Don't worry, I will

have no trouble getting loose when the change is complete. Do this for me, Oliver. Please."

He stood for a moment, staring at her. Then he went out through the curtain into the other room. From a cabinet under the sink he took a coil of stout nylon line and a hunting knife. He brought them back to the bed.

Irena lay on her back waiting for him. Silently he cut several pieces from the nylon line. He tied her wrists together, then lashed them to the metal bedstand above her head.

Irena watched intently as he finished the job, tying one of her ankles to each side of the metal footboard, spreading her legs. She was moist and ready for him.

"Now, my Oliver," she whispered, "make love to me for the last time ever."

He stripped off his clothes and lowered himself on top of her. She raised her head and kissed him eagerly. He slid easily into her. Irena made little mewing sounds as he withdrew a little bit, then thrust in again, withdrew, and thrust.

The bed jumped and creaked as Irena strained against the tough nylon bonds. Oliver had left enough slack for her to move her body about. He was overcome now with a raging need to have her. He pounded into her again and again, flesh slapping hard against flesh.

Irena hummed in his ear. The humming coarsened, became a growl. Without slowing his thrusts, Oliver raised his head to look down at her face. She smiled. The sharp white fangs curved out over her lips.

Oliver continued to pound into her until they erupted together in a fiery climax.

Irena raised her leopard head and roared.

Chapter 30

Oliver walked with Alice Moore along the Big Cat path in the New Orleans Zoo. Between them walked the young man who was hired to replace Joe Creigh as handler.

"Why do you want to get into this work?" Oliver asked the young man.

"Mostly, I just like animals." He grinned at Joe and turned to include Alice.

"A zoo isn't like a pet store, you know," Alice said.

"Hey, you don't have to remind me to respect these fellas. I read in the paper what happened to the guy who worked here before me."

"Doesn't that worry you?" Oliver asked.

The young man answered gravely. "I was raised on a farm, and I never saw an animal turn on a man without the man does something to hurt or frighten him. I figure this guy must have brought it on himself. Either that or he was Godawful careless."

"You've got the right attitude for the work," Oliver said. "I hope you keep it."

They walked down the row of cages, past the slumbering lions and the pacing tigers. At the end of the row, set apart from the others, was a new cage, larger than the rest. There was a pool of fresh water and a climbing tree inside. A cavelike tunnel at the rear led to an enclosed sleeping space.

"What do you keep in there?" the new handler asked.

"This is one cage I want you to stay completely away from," Oliver said. "I take care of this one personally."

From beyond the tunnel came a soft throaty growl.

Oliver looked past the young handler to Alice. "It's getting late, and I have things to do. You two go ahead and finish the tour without me."

"Right," Alice said crisply. She took the young man by the arm. "Let's go say hello to the bears."

Oliver watched until they were out of sight, then he turned and walked down the short path to the new cage. The soft growl came again. He stopped just outside the bars.

"I'm here," he said.

In flowing slow motion a sleek, beautifully formed black leopard emerged from the tunnel. The cat glided over to the bars where Oliver stood. The raised floor of the cage put its huge amber eyes on a level with his.

For many minutes the man and the cat faced each other silently, barely moving. Then Oliver put a hand in through the bars and stroked the animal's face.

"No one will ever hurt you again," he said. "I promise you."

The shadows lengthened and evening came. In couples and in families the people left the zoo. The daytime animals slept and the night birds took up their cry, and down at the end of the Big Cat path, the man stood alone with the leopard.